PARANORMAL COZY MYSTERY

Fatal Wines & Valentines

TRIXIE SILVERTALE

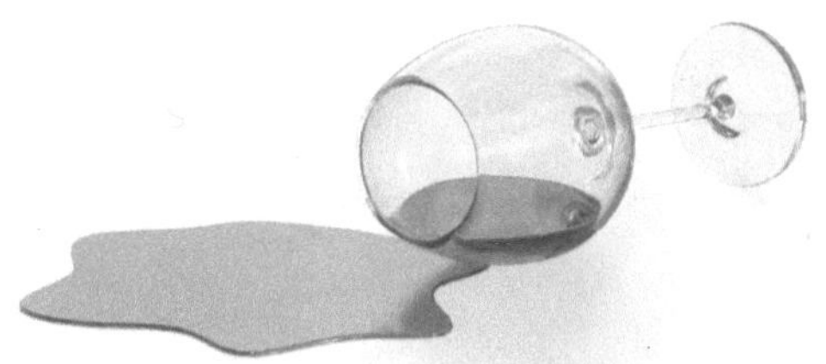

May you Power Tour through eternity,
my sweet boy...
You will never be forgotten.

Sittin' On A Goldmine Productions, L.L.C.

pr@sittinonagoldmine.co

www.sittinonagoldmine.co

ISBN: 978-1-952739-64-4

Cover design by Melony Paradise of Paradise Cover Design

Trixie Silvertale
Fatal Wines and Valentines: Paranormal Cozy Mystery : a novel / by Trixie Silvertale — 1st ed.
[1. Paranormal Cozy Mystery — Fiction. 2. Cozy Mystery —

Fiction. 3. Amateur Sleuths — Fiction. 4. Private Investigator — Fiction. 5. Wit and Humor — Fiction.] 1. Title.

PROLOGUE

CRASH!

A bone-chilling scream.

Erick runs toward the commotion, and I follow — instinctively.

Guests are scurrying left and right. Shouting. Panicking. Surviving.

Following my husband through the swinging door—

The scene before me defies logic.

What can we do? Are we too late?

Calm under pressure, Erick takes charge and I swallow my horror and struggle to help.

My senses are on overload. The pandemonium drains my psychic abilities.

Escaping the chaos in the winery, I dive into a

spacious private bathroom, lock the door behind me, and attempt to pull it together.

The reflection in the mirror has been through the wringer.

My perfect face-framing tendrils are sticking to the clammy skin of my cheeks, and tears have dragged streaks of mascara down my face.

When was I crying?

How did I get blood on my dress . . .?

CHAPTER 1

BING. BONG. BING.

"He's here!" Grams and I blurt out our knee-jerk response and then giggle like schoolgirls.

"I guess it's probably not Erick. You know, since we're married now, and he lives here."

Grams presses a bejeweled hand to her ample bosom and attempts to catch her nonexistent ghost-breath. "It's like that experiment. Was it Freud? With cats? No, that was Schrödinger . . ."

"It was Pavlov, and it was dogs. How 'bout you pull yourself together, and I'll get the door?"

Pressing the plaster medallion embossed with vines of twisted ivy, I wait for my secret bookcase door to glide open. As I pad softly across the thick, imported carpets of the Rare Books Loft, I brush my fingers along the perfectly aligned edges of the oak reading desks.

The books on the secured mezzanine hold the scent of mystery and wisdom.

Once a month, my volunteer employee, Twiggy, organizes scholastic research appointments, and we allow visitors to come up to the normally off-limits second-floor loft. In a busy month, all the small brass lamps with their handcrafted green glass shades glow brightly as book nerds soak in the knowledge coded into these ancient pages. This morning, only the weak light of the winter sun filters through the 6 x 6 slumped-glass panes at the front of the bookshop.

Wending my way down the metal steps of the wrought-iron circular staircase, I marvel at the beauty of my collection.

My grandmother has more than a knack for fashion. Her careful restoration and renovation of this historic brewery is truly a marvel. Tin-plated ceilings gleam above seemingly endless rows of books. The first floor contains traditional bookshelves in orderly lines, while the looming mezzanine maintains a whisper of the architecture that once curved around the large brewing vats.

As a lover of books, there are days when I have to pinch myself to be sure this isn't a dream. Although today feels mundane. Slow to start.

Passing the back room reveals two things. 1. Twiggy has not arrived. 2. Pyewacket's bowl is empty, and he's nowhere in sight.

Approaching the heavy metal door that serves as the delivery entrance for my store, I twist the lock and push open the door.

A blur of tan fur rockets past me, nearly knocking me over, and for a moment I wonder how and when my half-wild caracal learned to ring the doorbell.

However, before my mind can tumble down that road and twist itself into knots, a man who looks as though he's dropped through a time portal steps into view.

Tilted at a rakish angle, a spotless grey fedora adorns his head while the collar of his elegant worsted-wool overcoat is turned up against the howling winds.

You may assume that wind is a normal part of life, but this narrow alleyway that separates my home and store from my father's Restorative Justice Foundation funnels the icy blasts knifing across the great lake nestled in Pin Cherry's harbor into near weaponized weather.

"Madame, are you Mitzy Moon, proprietress of the Bell, Book & Candle Bookshop?"

Stifling a chuckle, I cross my arms over my reindeer onesie pajamas and attempt to look as professional as his title insinuates. "Yes, I'm Mitzy. We're not open yet. Is there something I can help you with, or would you like to come back?"

"My only wish is to put this directly into the hands of its intended."

The strange man extracts a gilded envelope from his deep pocket and extends it toward me.

I'm sure most of you would grab this envelope like Charlie grabbed Willy Wonka's golden ticket. But you probably haven't had nearly as many run-ins with dark magic, ghosts, and good old-fashioned murderers as I have. My history with misfortune gives me reason to hesitate.

The man patiently waits for me to take his golden missive.

Using one of the skills taught to me by my mentor, Silas Willoughby, I reach out with my extrasensory perceptions and confirm the envelope contains no whiff of ill will or dangerous alchemy.

Satisfying myself that all is clear, I take the envelope and offer an overdue smile. "Thank you. I haven't had my coffee yet this morning. I apologize. Appreciate the hand delivery, though. So rare these days."

As soon as I take the item, the man raises his black-leather-gloved hand and doffs his cap. He vanishes around the corner — never looking back.

The gesture with the fedora makes me think of

the adorable head nod that Erick generally offers when he's putting on his best manners or attempting to be extra official. Images of Detective Too-Hot-To-Handle dance in my head.

"RE-ow." Feed me.

Shoot! Back to reality. One thing a caracal never jokes about is his hunger. Turning toward my fiendish feline, I narrow my gaze. "If you—"

"Mitzy!" The ghost of my not-as-dead-as-everyone-thinks grandmother blasts through the wall and engulfs me in a warm hum of otherworldly energy.

"Easy, Casper. I have to feed His Majesty or suffer the consequences."

Pyewacket slowly rotates his black-tufted ears in my direction. "Reow." Can confirm.

Summoning the energy to affect matter in my dimension, Grams snatches the golden envelope from my hands. "You've finally arrived!"

Shambling toward the back room, I press the button on the cranky coffeemaker and retrieve the box of sugary children's cereal from the small pantry.

As I bend to fill Pye's bowl with his beloved Fruity Puffs, I grumble, "Arrived? What on earth are you ghost-squealing about? I've been here for almost four years. Not sure what I did for you to finally consider that an arrival."

I risk a hasty scratch between my furry overlord's ears before he begins his breakfast. Trust me, I've learned not to mess with the beast while he's eating.

"Mitzy, you're such a hoot. You know what I mean."

Grams presses the gleaming envelope to her burgundy silk-and-tulle Marchesa gown and spins like a jewelry-box ballerina.

Yeesh. Not awake enough to care.

A heavenly scent wafts my way.

Finally! Enough coffee in the pot to fill a cup. I yank it free, and dripping coffee hits the warming pad beneath the pot, hissing angrily. Filling a cup, I replace the pot and take a greedy gulp.

"Too hot! Too hot!" Fanning my mouth with one hand, I attempt to blow cool air over my tongue. Patience is not a lesson I'm destined to learn in this lifetime.

"Do you know what this is, Mitzy?" Her voice is practically in song.

"Myrtle Isadora, for the one-millionth time, no. I have no idea what it is. But I bet you're going to tell me."

Grams drifts dreamily from the back room and floats through the enormous chandelier dangling above the main floor, without disturbing a single crystal. She rides the weak beams of sunlight like one of the many dust motes thriving in our stacks.

"This is the most exclusive event in all of Pin Cherry Harbor. Scratch that, all of Birch County! He only invites forty people each year. Any idea how hard it is to get onto that guest list?"

Her excitement grows, and she loses the ability to hold the invitation.

The shimmering invite flutters toward the ground like a golden snitch running out of magic.

Plucking the formal letter from the air, I open the envelope and slide the luxurious creamy paper from its gilded prison.

"Read it out loud, dear!" Grams is positively buzzing.

"'Mizithra Achelois Moon, the honor of your presence is requested at Châteauneuf-du-Nord's annual Valentine's in the Vines Gala.' That's it, Grams. It doesn't say 'from whom.' There's no address. Not even a date. What the heck?"

Ghost-ma continues to glide above my head.

"Hey! You look like a ghost in the know. Who throws this party, and where do I get the rest of the details?"

Her ethereal glow brightens, and she seems to snap out of whatever reverie held her in its thrall.

"Oh, sweetie, you have all the information you need. A sleigh drawn by two gorgeous Friesian stallions will show up on Valentine's Day at sunset. The sleigh will take you to the winery and the indescribable festivities that await. You're in for the night of your life, my darling."

Funny how none of that was in the card. "Listen, I barely convinced myself to accept an envelope from someone I didn't know. After all the shenanigans I've had to deal with, there's no way I'm getting into a sleigh that's taking me to an undisclosed location. Who owns this winery? Who is throwing this party?"

Ghost-ma whooshes toward me, but as she draws near, her aura flickers. She pauses several feet from me, and her ghostly image jumps like the tracking on an old VHS tape.

"Grams! Are you all right? You look really weird."

She clutches at one of her many strands of pearls and gasps. "I can't remember his name. It's a complete blank. I held the record for most invitations, and now—"

"Don't worry, Grams. It's all the excitement. The special-delivery invite, all this talk about parties. It's only a temporary glitch. Why don't you head up to the closet in my old apartment and start working on my wardrobe for the gala?"

For a moment, her chosen appearance as a thirty-five-year-old ghost fades. I see the true age of the woman who died years ago in her sixties — complete with subsequent decomp. Well, that's new. And unsettling.

A spasm of shivers grip my body. "I'm gonna take a cup of coffee to Erick. Down at the — our office. I can't wait to see what you pick out for me."

There's no way I'll risk letting her see me cry. Holding my mind blank, so she can't read my thoughts, I rush through the "Employees Only" door into the remodeled walk-up and throw a parka over my reindeer onesie pajamas. Once I add snow boots and a stocking hat, no one will be the wiser. As I run-walk toward the offices of Harper and Moon Investigations, one thought consumes all others . . .

I have to call Silas immediately. He'll know what to do about Grams.

CHAPTER 2

TRUDGING THROUGH THE ANKLE-DEEP SNOW, I have to admit winter is growing on me. I've always been a fan of seasons, but there's a sizeable difference between winter in the high desert of the Southwest and winter at this latitude. It was one heckuva gear change to go from a couple days of fluffy snow that would easily melt away, to mountains and mountains of the white stuff that have to be cleared by enormous plows.

Blerg! In my rush to leave the walk-up, I completely spaced the cover story about coffee. Oh well, hopefully, my ready smile will be enough for Mr. Harper.

Pushing open the door to our PI office, I stomp the snow off my boots and toss my leather choppers and stocking hat onto the side table. When I turn to accept my husband's welcoming embrace, I receive quite a shock.

And yes, even psychics get caught off guard.

Erick's face is a mask of surprise tinged with guilt, and the woman sitting next to him in the waiting area with a steaming cup of coffee wears a smirk I don't appreciate.

Quick as a flash, Erick is on his feet, stuttering out an explanation.

"Mitzy! I didn't— Did you—? Good morning."

I stiffly accept my expected hug and place a fist on my hip.

His eyes slip across my person, and it's only then I remember I'm still wearing my pajamas and never bothered to yank a comb through my haystack of snow-white hair.

All the sass drains away like sands through an hourglass, as my cheeks blush profusely. I whisper, "I didn't know you were entertaining."

He swipes a sexy hand across his furrowed brow and swallows with difficulty.

"Mitzy, this is an old high school friend, Antoinette Pearson." He amps up the wattage on his smile. "Nettie, this is my wife, Mitzy."

The smirk remains on Nettie's face as she walks toward me and extends one hand.

In general, I'm not a fan of handshakes, but I'm struggling to get a hold of this greased pig of a situation, so I accept her hand and note fingernails bitten to the quick and several calluses.

Erick's voice maintains an unnatural cheeriness. "So, Nettie wants to hire us." He nods like a young parent attempting to convince a toddler that vegetables are yummy. "There've been a couple of strange accidents out at the winery, and last week an entire shipment of grapes from South America vanished. She'd like someone to take an official look. Isn't that great?"

"Winery? This wouldn't happen to be Châteauneuf-du-Nord, would it?"

He gnaws on his bottom lip, and it doesn't take a psychic to tell he's worried I'm having a vision.

Nettie sniffs sharply and scrapes a loose strand of her velvet black hair back into her loose ponytail. "Yes. It's my family's winery. Why do you ask?"

Enjoying my brief moment in the sun, I delay my direct response. "Seems like we'll need some type of cover story to legitimately poke around the property without raising suspicion, right?"

She nods silently while Erick fidgets his weight from one foot to the other.

"Well, I have just the thing. I received an invitation to the Valentine's in the Vines Gala this morning."

Either Erick is unfazed by this news or has no idea what gala I'm talking about.

Nettie, on the other hand, takes a step backward and appears to have some bile, or possibly a crumb of her "upper crust", caught in her throat. "You?" Her eyes drag across me. "You were invited?"

Other than her obvious judgment of my current appearance, I love everything about this moment. "Yes." I follow up with the "official" story of my genealogy. "I'm the granddaughter of Myrtle Isadora and Cal Duncan." At the mention of my notorious grandmother and railroad-tycoon grandfather, Antoinette's demeanor shifts rapidly.

"Oh my gosh! You're Cal Duncan's granddaughter? He and my dad were hunting buddies. Drinking buddies. And poker buddies. Sorry for the—"

"I don't usually leave the house like this." Gesturing to my reindeer onesie, I continue. "I had an urgent matter to discuss with my *husband* and didn't expect anyone to be here at this hour." The tone of my voice is not lost on my observant partner.

Erick places a hand on Nettie's shoulder, and I slip around the pair to get myself another cup of joe, while totally eavesdropping.

"Thanks for thinking of us, Nettie. I'll take a look at the information about the gala with Mitzy. But this sounds like the perfect cover. Let me know if anything happens before Wednesday, but it seems like we have a good plan moving forward. I'll be in touch about our retainer."

Nettie grips his hand with her thick fingers and pumps it vigorously. "Thanks, Ricky. I knew I could count on you. At some point, I'm going to convince my father that I'm the right *son* to run that winery. I'd like there to be something left when I do."

He removes his hand from her shoulder and crosses his arms over his chest in that way that makes his biceps bulge. But I'm not pleased someone else stands in the prime viewing location.

"So after everything you've done ol' Cromwell is still trying to shove this thing down Leon's throat?" Erick shakes his head and exhales heavily.

She slaps her leather mittens into the palm of her opposite hand and shrugs. "You know Napoleon, always obsessed with his physics. Even got his master's degree in the stuff. He does just enough to keep Dad off his back, but nowhere near what it takes to actually run a winery. Emmanuel and I were always more interested than Leon. But the great Cromwell Pearson insists on handing everything off to his eldest son."

Erick pats her on the shoulder as she exits. "Sorry to hear that, Nettie. Hopefully, we'll find out more about these accidents, and maybe that will give you a leg up with your dad."

She chuckles and shakes her head. “Sure, and Hell might freeze over, Ricky.”

He closes the door behind her. I shake my head as he sheepishly approaches.

“Ricky, Ricky, Ricky. I leave you alone for five minutes, and here you are trying to reignite some high school romance.”

He pulls my cup of coffee from my hand and sets it on a nearby filing cabinet as he drags me into a snug embrace. “I’d be offended if I didn’t know you were kidding. Nettie was on the football team with me, okay? First girl to play for the Pin Cherry Harbor high school team. She’s made of tough stuff. So, for her to be concerned enough to come here asking for help— Well, I’m worried something nefarious might actually be going on out there.”

Inhaling his citrus-woodsy scent, I gaze up into his gentle blue eyes. “Nefarious, you say. Oh, dear. I expect Harper and Moon better get on the case as quickly as possible.”

Before I can unleash any additional snark, he plants a lovely kiss on my expectant mouth.

“I like it when you’re jealous, Moon. Your grey eyes sparkle with that same mischief I remember from the first day I saw you at Myrtle’s Diner.”

Snaking my arms around his neck, I tilt my head. “You mean the day you pulled me into a horizontal embrace?”

His rugged features instantly blush.

Yep. Still got it.

"I remember it differently." His gaze softens with emotion. "You tripped and fell on *me*."

Erick hugs me close, and we share laughter over the memory of our "meet cute."

As a film-school dropout, I find it incredibly satisfying when a movie trope pays off. And that "meet cute" turned out better than any Hallmark movie I've ever watched.

He releases me from the embrace and returns the coffee mug to my hand. "So, what's this gala you mentioned?"

"Honestly, I have about as much information as you. Some well-dressed messenger showed up this morning and delivered a strange golden envelope. Grams nearly— Crapballs! Seeing you with Nettie made me forget the entire reason I came down here." Pulling my phone out of the pocket in my parka, I continue. "To get privacy. I need to call Silas. I'll put him on speaker, and you can listen as I explain it all to him."

"10-4."

Time to call my lawyer, and alchemy mentor, Silas Willoughby.

"Good morning, Mr. Willoughby. I hope you slept well."

There's a distinct harrumph, and it's all too easy

to picture him smoothing his bushy grey mustache with a thumb and forefinger. “Good morning, Mitzy. How is your day progressing?”

First, I let him know he’s on speaker with me and Erick, and then I bring him up to speed on the events of the morning. “So, I’m really starting to get worried about Grams. She seems to be getting weaker and super forgetful.”

There’s a lengthy pause, but finally, his scholarly voice fills the room. “I admit, I too have witnessed these episodes. I am unable to observe her as frequently as you, Mizithra. But with the aid of my alchemically altered spectacles and the use of the 3 x 5 cards to obtain Isadora’s side of the story, I have made note of a shift. If she were still on this plane, I’d simply attribute it to the ravages of time. Being that she remains on our side of the veil, residing between here and there, with a tether holding her to your bookshop, these events are unprecedented. I must conduct in-depth research.”

Worry pinches my shoulders together. “You’ll figure something out, right? There’s gotta be a way to re-energize her, or . . .”

“The universe is populated by absolutes, hypotheses, and ever-changing ideas. I shall attempt to collect data that may serve to tip the scales in our favor.”

Leave it to Silas to offer the most vague reply

possible. "Copy that."

After ending the call, I turn to Erick, give him a head-to-toe once over, and shake my head.

His expression turns oddly self-conscious. "What? You don't like my hair? I thought you liked the slicked-back-with-pomade look."

"Oh, it's not me you'll have to impress. Currently, Grams is using every last sparkle of her energy to plan my wardrobe for the gala. But if you think you'll be immune from her critical gaze, you're dreaming, Detective."

He straightens his collar and rakes his fingers through his blond hair. "Isadora loves me. What are you talking about?"

"Hey, you got off easy at the wedding, buster. She doesn't have an enormous party-planning list to distract her this time. Once she finishes with my gown, shoes, hairdo, and jewels . . . She'll be coming for you."

Erick's eyes widen as he gulps. "Help?"

I snicker, take a slow pull on my coffee, and shrug. I'm going to enjoy this. "Let's head over to the diner Grams inspired and get a proper breakfast before we have to face the fashion maven. What do you say?"

He hands me my hat and mittens and makes a small bow. "After you, M'lady."

Oh brother.

CHAPTER 3

My soul enjoys having a touchstone like Myrtle's Diner. Walking in, being embraced by familiar scents and sounds, and receiving a spatula salute from Odell, or, as I like to call him, Gramps, makes it feel as though everything is right in the world.

Following Erick to our usual booth in the corner, I'm working my way across the red-vinyl bench seat when the world's best waitress, Tally, arrives bearing two steaming mugs of black gold.

"Morning, kids. Got any new cases this week?"

Erick shrugs, but I'm eager to spill a little gossip into the local pipeline. "I got an invitation to Cromwell Pearson's Valentine's Day Gala." I pause and allow her to offer the appropriate gasp before continuing. "I bet I'm allowed a plus one. Who do you think I should take?"

Tally's mouth slowly opens like the door on a creaky old mailbox. Her eyes widen, and I worry she may drop the pot of coffee.

"I'm just kidding, Tally! Of course I'm taking Erick."

She presses a free hand to her chest and takes several shallow breaths as her usual smile jumps back into place. Tally nods her flame-red topknot back and forth while she chuckles. "You got me. You definitely got me that time, Mitzy." With a final grin, she hurries toward the counter to refill more mugs with the diner's signature blend of delicious java.

Hijacking my move, Erick walks his fingers across the table and turns his palm upward.

I slide my hand into his, and little tingles race up my arm as he squeezes my hand and rubs his thumb back and forth across my fingers. "So you really think your grandmother is gonna get involved in my wardrobe? Can't I just wear any old tuxedo?"

Luckily, my mug is still inches from my mouth. Otherwise, there would've been a good old-fashioned coffee spit take all over this silver-flecked white Formica table. "Any old tuxedo? Let me give you a helpful tip when dealing with Myrtle Isadora. Never, and I mean *never ever*, refer to couture as 'any old.' If you have a tuxedo, you better bring it to the apartment for her inspection. It may pass muster, but be prepared for pocket squares, bow ties, shinier shoes, and I have no idea what else. I'm only speaking from my years of experience, Lovebug."

A smile lifts his cheeks as he laughs lightly. "Just a little over six weeks from our anniversary . . . Was that a pet name I heard?"

I roll my eyes, rub a hand over my face, and slump my shoulders in defeat. "I know! I know! I said no silly pet names. And I almost made it the entire year, but I might have to admit you were right about something."

He withdraws his hand, sits back, and laces his fingers together behind his head as he prepares to enjoy his momentary victory.

Of course, that gesture immediately causes my eyes to dart toward his washboard abs, on the off chance that his maneuver will tug his shirt up just enough to offer me a peek.

His laughter deepens as he leans across the table and envelops both of my hands in his. "If we're splitting hairs, Moon, I'd have to say Detective Too-Hot-To-Handle is a bit of a pet name. So I don't think you followed your own rules for even a day."

Blerg.

"Touché, Harper. Touché."

Odell arrives and places my favorite scrambled

eggs with chorizo and a side of golden-brown home fries in front of me. As he sets the required bottle of Tabasco on the table, my face scrunches up in confusion. "Gramps, where are Erick's blueberry pancakes?"

He and Erick exchange an unreadable glance, and my grandfather's coffee-brown eyes twinkle with mischief when he looks back at me. "Not everyone has the luxury of sleeping till noon, kid."

"Noon? It's only 10:30 a.m. Are you telling me Erick has already been here and had breakfast this morning?"

Odell smirks, raps his knuckles twice on our table, and strides back to his domain. Learning the truth of my father's parentage and reuniting Odell and Grams was a magical moment. However, time doesn't stand still for the living. Maybe that has something to do with what's bothering Grams. My eyes follow him and I shake my head. "Did he get a haircut? I mean, I know he always has the buzz cut, but the buzz seems a little closer to the skin. Maybe even a little more salt than pepper these days." My voice trails off.

My partner takes a sip of his coffee and shrugs. "That's the kind of thing you would notice. I only notice that his hair is always sat and never touches the ears."

"Sat?" Arching one eyebrow, I await an explanation.

"'Sat' is the military term for satisfactory. It means within regulations."

I nod my understanding of the term, not necessarily of the military. My grandfather served decades before Erick and technically outranks him. However, their mutual respect for the Army and each other doesn't hinge on rank.

"Entertain me while I power through this breakfast, hubby."

He drums his fingertips on the table. "Let's see . . . I'll need a story that will last roughly five minutes."

"Erick!"

"Hey, I say it out of admiration, not judgment."

I tuck into my delicious fare while Erick attempts to fascinate me with an anecdote about high school football. Honestly, I catch a few names, and smile when he chuckles, but ninety-nine percent of my attention is with the food. I wouldn't go so far as to say breakfast is the most important meal of the day — I don't play favorites with my mealtimes — but there's something divine about home fries cooked to perfection.

Wiping my mouth, I utter a sigh of satisfaction and push my mug toward the edge of the table for a refill.

Erick leans back, tilts his head, and asks, "Well, what do you think? Sound like a good idea?"

Temporary panic grips me, and for a split second, I worry he'll discover my lack of attention. Thank goodness for psychic abilities. Pressing mental "replay" on the previous conversation, I quickly realize he's yanking my chain. "Nice try, Harper. You didn't ask me anything. I believe that qualifies as attempted entrapment."

He laughs, but his eyes drift from me to whoever just walked in the door.

The stomp of boots is followed by, "Hey, Sheriff. I mean, Harper."

"You picking up doughnuts for the station, Deputy Johnson?"

"More like I'm *buying* doughnuts for the station."

Erick slides out of the booth and approaches the counter where Tally is loading sugary pastries into an obligatory pink box.

"What happened?"

Deputy Johnson shakes his head. "Oh, you know. I did something to get on Paulsen's bad side, and I'm hoping these doughnuts will keep me from having to write parking tickets at the community college parking lot all day."

Erick chuckles and places a hand on his former deputy's shoulder. "I remember when I came up with that consequence. Glad to see it carries on even though I'm no longer sheriff."

Johnson laughs and shakes his head. "Yeah, thanks for that, eh?"

Erick points to the box. "If you want to get on Paulsen's good side, you better make sure there's a bear claw in there. And, Tally, you can put those doughnuts on my tab."

Tally smiles from ear to ear. "You betcha. Just between us, you were the best sheriff this town ever had."

He waves away the compliment with a self-deprecating gesture, but Johnson chimes in. "She's right, Harper. We all miss you at the station, but I'm glad to have you and Mrs. Moon working cases in town."

Erick nods his head in that way that insinuates he's doffing a cap, and returns to our table.

Rather than slide out of the booth and put my reindeer onesie on display for the local deputy, I sit tight and allow Erick to rejoin me in the booth.

"Now who's playing fast and loose with the heiress money, Harper?"

He chuckles. "Hey, I always pay for breakfast out of my personal account, Your Highness."

A little flush touches my cheeks as I smile at the kindhearted man across from me. "Have I told you how much I love you?"

He reaches for my hands, looks directly into my eyes, and whispers, "Not today. Plus, I prefer when you *show me.*"

And I'm dead.

While the coast is clear, we bundle up and trudge back to the walk-up. From the sidewalk, I can see the corner of an envelope poking from the top of our antique mailbox affixed to the brick wall beside the entrance.

"Look, we have mail!"

Erick chuckles and holds the front door for me while I retrieve the post. Once inside, he strides across the open-plan kitchen, dining room, living room, and adds more logs to the glowing embers in the fireplace. "Anything good?"

"Junk mail." Pulling out the hidden waste bin, I chuck the ad for winter excavating services into the trash. "Why don't you head over to your old place and pick up that tux you're so proud of, while I sacrifice myself on the altar of high fashion?" Glancing upward, I point in the direction of my old apartment at the back of the building and widen my eyes.

Erick stretches widely and yawns. "Maybe I'll drive with the windows open and see if I can freeze out this exhaustion."

I'm by his side in a flash. "What's wrong? Are you not sleeping?"

He shrugs his muscular shoulders. “I’m sleeping, but — It feels like I’m not rested. It doesn’t make sense.”

“Should I ask Silas if he has a tincture or—”

“Nah. It’ll pass. Don’t worry about it.” Erick shakes his head as he waves away my concern. “I’ll grab that tux and return in time for a fashion show.” His lips part, and he waggles his eyebrows.

“Now you’re pandering to Ghost-ma! Go on. Get outta here. And no more mention of fashion shows.” I swat at his behind, but he’s already strides ahead.

“Tell Isadora I’d like to see something strapless.” He laughs as I lunge toward the closing door.

Trying to convince myself it won’t be that bad, I swallow hard and paste on a fake smile.

Time to see how out of hand things have gotten with Grams.

CHAPTER 4

I SHUFFLE THROUGH THE DOOR from the empty walk-up, between the stacks on the first floor, and attempt to hop over the "No Admittance" chain hooked across the bottom of the circular staircase.

Distraction wins the day, and I lurch forward, banging my knee harshly on a metal step.

"Sweetie! Oh, that will leave a nasty bruise. You'll certainly have to wear a full-length gown now."

Before I can admonish Grams for her misplaced concerns, the cackle of my volunteer employee fills the room and echoes off the tin-plated ceiling.

"Consider me paid in full for this week, doll. Speaking of, I'm about to place the supply order. You need any more green yarn for that murder board of yours?"

My reply catches in my throat when the front door opens, and the silhouette of Silas Willoughby takes shape.

"Silas? You didn't mention you were headed this way. Is everything all right?"

He pulls the door closed and knocks the excess snow from his boots. "I mentioned research, did I not?"

"Oh, right." An attempt to get to my feet is unsuccessful. "Ouch. Ow! Shoot, I really cracked my knee on that step."

Twiggy flicks her severe grey pixie cut and shoves her hands into the pockets of her dungarees. "I'll order more green yarn just to be safe. Silas can take care of that knee." And with that, she stomps her biker boots into the back room, and I wriggle under the chain to perch on the bottom step of the circular staircase. "Can you do anything about it?"

Silas adjusts his mystery-stained bowtie, harrumphs, and crouches in front of me. He places his left hand on my banged-up knee and mumbles under his pipe-tobacco-scented breath.

In the past, I've generally ignored his mumbling, but over time, I've learned great power resides in his secret phrases.

Turning up my clairaudience, I hope to catch a snippet of his alchemy at work.

When my brain registers the phrase "Magic

hand. Magic hand. Magic hand," I can't contain my shock and awe.

"Magic? You told me you don't do magic, Silas. You told me it was all alchemical workings and transmutations. What's a *magic hand*?"

A smile deepens the lines around his rheumy blue eyes as he pats my knee and retrieves the small stool from between the stacks. "I did not develop the wording for this working, Mizithra."

Uh oh. Formal name territory. That can only mean one thing. A lesson.

"The incantation was developed by my late brother, Jedediah. He selected the word impulsively. Due, in no small part, to the fact that it worked — as any mortal would describe — magically."

"Can you teach me? I'm kind of accident-prone. Something like this might come in handy."

"I must admit, I'm surprised to hear your inaugural idea is one composed solely of self. Historically, your heart has been more outward facing."

"It came out wrong, Silas. Of course I would use it to help others. It's just that — in between helping others — I might have a chance to use it on myself once in a while."

"Indeed." He harrumphs and sweeps the topic away with a fluid motion. "I must lead you into a deep trance and place the working within your psyche. Are you amenable to this?"

"Sure. Knock yourself out." As soon as the words escape my mouth, I regret them. "I mean, I'm ready to accept the responsibility of this potent alchemical knowledge. Proceed."

That receives a chuckle from my venerable mentor. His ruddy cheeks glow and his hangdog jowls shake with laughter.

A snort from Ghost-ma joins the general mockery, and Pye creeps into the shadows beneath the staircase.

"I shall retrieve a bag of beans from the children's section. It would behoove you to be reclined, relaxed, and not in a position where you could cause yourself injury."

Bag of beans?

Oh! As he grabs the new beanbag chair from the children's section under the mezzanine, I call out, "You have my full attention, Mr. Willoughby."

When he returns, I transfer myself, with less pain than earlier, to the beanbag.

Silas pulls his rose-tinted, wire-rimmed eyeglasses from an inner pocket of his fusty tweed coat. He tugs the curved bows over his preternaturally large ears and gazes at Grams. "It would be best if you left us, Isadora. This working requires intense concentration."

"Well, I never . . ." Grams floats toward the apartment.

Eager to get on with things, I adapt the message. "Grams is happy to oblige."

A tinkle of laughter echoes in her wake.

"Excellent. We shall begin. Close your eyes and focus on a point far beyond your heavy lids. Visualize the numeral three. Visualize yourself writing the number three on a chalkboard three times. Now, visualize the number two. Scribe that number on the chalkboard three times."

His voice is low and steady. Soothing. All-encompassing.

"And now the numeral one. Again, scratching the chalk across the board as you write the number one, three times. Your eyelids are heavy. Your limbs are heavy."

Relaxation floods my body. It feels as though I'm floating on a cloud.

"You now see yourself at the top of a staircase. You must hold the wooden railing with your hand and walk down the stairs as you count down from ten.

"Deeper and deeper.

"Nine. Sinking as your hand slides down the polished wood.

"Eight, seven. Deeper and deeper."

His voice is a gentle hum in the far recesses of my mind.

"You're drifting into peacefulness.

"Six, five. Deeper and deeper.

"Four, three. Deeper and deeper.

"Two, one. You are fully relaxed."

I've never felt so peaceful.

The tranquilizing murmur of his voice continues. "There is a door in front of you. The door appears any way you choose. Open the door and step inside.

"Inside this room, you see only a bucket on a pedestal. Approach the pail and gaze into the water.

"The bucket is filled with ice water — so cold there is condensation on the exterior of the metal pail. You must plunge your arm into the bucket past your elbow, and hold it firm."

I thrust my arm into the bucket. The intense cold bites into my flesh. "It's cold. It's so cold."

The reassuring voice of my mentor continues. "You cannot be hurt. You cannot suffer. Allow the ice to penetrate your very bones. Feel the chill and the burn alternating. Heat and cold, taking each cell in your limb to a place beyond pain."

At first, I struggle to feel beyond the spikes of icy pain, but as I focus on Mr. Willoughby's voice, I can envision heat and cool, and, moving beyond them, I finally reach the place where the pain vanishes.

"You have created a clean slate. A surface free from pain, removed from suffering. You may invoke this magic hand to remove pain and to stop bleeding. You simply hold the left hand aloft and say, 'I invoke magic hand. Magic hand. Magic hand. Take away the pain. Stop the bleeding. Magic hand. Magic hand. Magic hand.'"

The words seem to be scribed into my bones. I can never forget them. The alchemy is part of me now.

"Remove your arm from the bucket and note this: if ever you need to transfer the working from the left hand to the right, you need only touch the left fingertips to the palm of your right hand and say, 'I transfer the magic hand.'"

In my vision, I feel the working move from one hand to the other, with ease.

"The working is complete. You may open your eyes when you are ready."

In the distance, there seems to be a snapping of fingers, or possibly a soft clap of hands. Either way, my eyelids roll open as I stare at Silas with a slack jaw and a racing pulse. "That's amazing. Did it work?"

He steeples his fingers and bounces his chin on the tip of his pointers.

Ah. The lesson is not complete. I hover my left hand above my banged-up left knee and repeat the mantra.

Within seconds, the pain in my knee vanishes completely.

"*Patch Adams*!" Pushing myself from the low-to-the-ground beanbag, I throw my arms around his neck and kiss his jowly cheek. "Thank you. I don't wish ill on anyone, but I'm looking forward to having an opportunity to use this to help someone else."

He chuckles lightly and returns the stool from whence it came. "I shall be in the Loft amongst the tomes. I would ask that you leave me undisturbed while I conduct my research."

"You betcha." I say this aloud, even though I'm currently following him up to said loft. Don't worry, I'm not going to bug him. I have other business.

Waiting for the secret bookcase door to slide open, I sense a presence behind me. Not Silas. This energy has a nosy, otherworldly vibe.

"Grams? Grams? If you're hiding just out of the physical spectrum, you can go ahead and manifest. I know you heard what we were talking about."

With a sharp crackle of electricity, Ghost-ma pops into view

"Technically, I wasn't eavesdropping, dear. I

was nearby in case there might be something I could do to help."

"I'm fine. My knee is fine, even fabulous. The only thing you need to do is conserve your energy. You'll have to stop working so hard on your memoirs — which we both know are actually about my life. Maintaining corporeal form and holding your quill pen takes a ton of your life force, or whatever you call it, to manifest on the physical plane."

"Nonsense. That's nothing. And you don't need to give another moment's thought to the memoirs. I sold them to a publisher!"

"You did what!?"

"Oh, don't get a bee in your bonnet, sweetie. We talked about this. I sent out a number of query letters, and, thanks to your adorable stepbrother Stellen, I got all my files in the proper format. Tah dah, success! I'm going to be published!"

Oh brother. There will be no living with her now.

"I heard that!" Grams places a bejeweled fist on her curvy hip.

"Is that so? Then you were clearly breaking the rules! No. Thought. Dropping."

"Oh, sweetie. I get so jumble—"

"Don't you start with me. If you expect me to support you selling my life story to some publisher, it's the least you can do to allow me a hot minute to be salty about it."

"There's no need to get huffy. I changed the names, as you asked." She crosses her arms and flutters her eyelashes.

"Whatever. Honestly, I have so much more to worry about right now. If it's like most books, it'll lie dormant on the shelf somewhere and never see a second printing."

"You could as least pretend to be happy for me." She sniffles with emotion.

"You're right. I'm sorry. I am happy for you, Grams. I wish the stories weren't about me, but I'm proud of you. You set your mind to something, and you completed it. Maybe now that you're not using so much energy working on the memoirs, you'll start to feel better."

Her aura flickers, and she struggles to wipe the concern from her features. "Yes, I'm sure you're right, dear."

"Now, I'm going to leave you to your duties in the closet, if you don't mind. I need to head over to the walk-up and try to distract myself from magic hands and memoirs with some obsessive cleaning."

Ghost-ma clutches one of her many strands of pearls and pretends to faint.

"Ha ha. I clean. You act like you've never seen

me pick up after myself. I can be very orderly when I plan for it. Right, Pye?"

Pyewacket's golden orbs fill with what can only be described as mirth, and then his eyelids squeeze tightly closed.

"What do I have to do to—? Never mind."

Tromping down the staircase, I risk triggering the alarm, and unhook the "No Admittance" chain. Even though I learned a nifty technique for reducing pain, I don't need to tempt fate twice in one day.

I secure the chain behind me before the alarm goes off. Whew!

A disembodied voice calls out from the back room. "You're finally getting the hang of things, kid. Maybe I should change the delay from thirty seconds to twenty and see if you're up to the challenge." Twiggy's cackle resounds through the bookshop, as I march into the walk-up to practice domesticity until my knight in a shiny copper Nova returns.

CHAPTER 5

When the door finally swooshes open, I'm fluffing the last of the multiple pillow shams on the king-size bed, way up in the primary suite.

"Erick! You're back!" That must be one heckuva tuxedo he fetched from his old place.

Thundering down the stairs, past the second-floor reading nook, I hurry into the living room, gasping for breath.

He's taking off his boots, and the expression on his face is wistful and distracted. "Hey. Would you mind ordering from Angelo and Vinci's for dinner?"

"No problem." Not sure whether he's going to want to talk about what's got him down, but what he needs right now is some delicious Italian comfort food. I can absolutely make that happen.

A quick call to Dante, the owner's son, sets up a

delivery of two portions of their amazing lasagna, a basket of garlic bread, and a bottle of Chianti. "Dinner is handled. Is there anything else I can do for you? Can I make you a cocktail? Or give you a neck rub?"

My Donna Reed impression finally breaks the ice.

Erick chuckles, walks toward me, and pulls me close.

"You know what would make me really happy right now?"

The way his arms encircle my waist and the smoky look in his eyes cause my heartbeat to increase. "Not exactly."

He chuckles. "Why don't we head over to the apartment and you can put on a little fashion show for me while we wait for Dante to deliver our supper?"

I can't be certain, but it feels like the color drains from my face. "You want to look at a bunch of silly gowns?"

He leans down and whispers so close to my ear that his lips brush my skin, sending tingles racing across my shoulders. "It's not the dresses I want to see on parade."

Gulp. "I'm starting to see why Isadora is so fond of you."

He snickers wickedly, takes my hand, and leads

the way through the bookshop up to my old apartment. Erick pulls the candle handle and waits with more patience than I've ever imagined possessing.

"Grams! Grams! I have fabulous news."

In the blink of an eye, my grandmother blasts through the wall next to the secret bookcase door. Her disembodied head, grinning maniacally, sends a chill of an entirely different kind down my spine. "Hey! Dial it down a notch, Beetlejuice."

Ignoring my quip, she reaches her glowing fingers toward me and attempts to manifest enough corporeal form to grab my hand. "News? Is it a great-grandchild?"

"Simmer down. Erick would like me to model the gowns you've selected for the gala tomorrow night."

Her glowing eyes widen to saucers, and she claps her hands like an over-excited pageant mom. "That man is one in a million, Mitzy."

"Yeah. He knows." I blow a loud breath through my lips and shake my head.

"Tell him to have a seat on the settee, dear. That will give him the best viewing experience." She taps one perfectly manicured finger on her coral lip, tilts her head, and nods in agreement with herself. "And you meet me in the closet, young lady."

Passing Ghost-ma's instructions along to Erick, I shuffle toward the massive closet.

There are five gowns carefully displayed around the space, and I can instantly rule out two. However, my current mission is to distract my wonderful husband and hopefully lull him into talking about his feelings. So I will put on whatever foolish contraption Grams tells me and pretend it's the happiest moment of my life.

"Where do I begin?" I can only hope my feigned excitement sounds believable.

"Let's start with the strapless white number. I think it's a little too bland for a winter gala, but it has a Snow Princess feel." She giggles uproariously at her own nod to last year's engagement hoopla.

"Copy that. White strapless it is." Having learned a thing or two from my fashion-forward ghost and the dearly departed tailor, Rivail Gustafson, I retrieve a bustier from one of the built-in drawers. Modeling isn't as easy a business as you might think.

Fortunately — for my grandmother, that is — Erick is as enamored with her selections as she is.

Teetering out of the closet in my four-inch silver slingbacks, I attempt a runway model walk, trip over my own clumsy feet, and fall into the arms of the ever-ready Mr. Harper.

"You're a knockout, Moon. I'm a little worried about the shoes, though." Once he sets me right, I return to the closet in mock shame.

When I lower onto the padded mahogany bench in the center of the museum of fashion, Pyewacket leaps up beside me and drops a slip of paper.

"What's this, buddy?" As I retrieve the item, Grams turns ghostly white — like, for real.

"A receipt?" My gaze darts to the total. "Who spent $800.00 on Coddled Couture?" My pointed stare falls on Myrtle Isadora.

"It was a once-in-a-lifetime find — and in your size, sweetie." A pleading glow emanates from her eyes.

"Grams, I love you — you know how much I love you — but your lifetime ended a few years ago. There are more than enough gowns in this closet to last me several lifetimes. You and Pye need to kick your online shopping habit. Understood?" My fist rests on my curvy hip as I await compliance.

She sheepishly grins. "Technically, it is my money, dear."

"WAS your money. I'll ask Silas to set a monthly budget for you. How does that sound?"

Her glowing eyes roll back. "A lot like husband number three, if you must know."

"Grandpa Cal? If memory serves, he was your second favorite. I'll take it."

When I attempt to discard the receipt, Pye

places a paw on the paper and gazes at me with disappointment.

"Fine. I'll hang onto it. It must be evidence of something other than the nonsense you and Grams get up to.

"Reow." Can confirm.

"Hey, is there more to this show, ladies?" Erick calls jokingly from the outer room.

"Yeah. Keep your shorts on, Harper."

Gesturing to Ghost-ma, we get the show back on the road.

The next two are barely worth mentioning, although there was the bonus of a two-inch heel with the pink chiffon number, which had three pounds of tissue paper stuffed inside to maintain its "shape" in the closet.

"Try on the red crepe, sweetie. I think that asymmetrical hemline and the one-shoulder draped neckline will look fabulous on you."

"Shockingly, I like that one, Grams. Who's the designer?"

She claps excitedly. "Oh, marvelous. That's circa 1970s vintage! The designer was Luis—Oh, it's on the tip of my tongue. Shoot." Ghost-ma swirls in tight circles, biting her lower lip.

"Don't worry about it." It's a struggle to keep my own concerns about her fading strength hidden behind a blank wall in my mind. Luckily, she's too distracted to notice.

"He designed gowns for Marilyn Monroe. Is it Luis Esteban? No."

"Honestly, Grams, the best thing to do is stop thinking about it. As soon as you relax, it will pop right in there."

She pauses and nods, but her aura flickers with doubt. "Try those shoes, dear."

Ghost-ma paired red patent leather Christian Louboutin pumps with a delicate ankle strap, with this vintage couture. The shimmering shoes have a slightly chunky heel and offer me the kind of stability I'm looking for in a high-heeled evening.

Stepping from the closet, I strike a pose and then offer a spin.

Erick rises to his feet and claps with wild abandon. "That's it. That's the one!" He glances around the room as though he might suddenly gain the ability to see the ghost of my grandmother. "Well done, Isadora. That's the winner."

Before my grandmother can reply—

BING. BONG. BING.

Erick raises a finger and grins. "I'll get the food. I'd tell you to leave the dress on, but it will be useless to us covered in tomato sauce."

As he exits the apartment, I shout in his wake. "Rude."

Changing into my far more comfortable skinny jeans and T-shirt helps me breathe a sigh of relief. This little tee has an empty wineglass tilted outward with the tagline, "Be kind. Please re-WINE." Seems appropriate for the occasion.

The delicious aroma of garlic bread arrives ahead of Erick.

"That smells so good." My tummy growls and I eagerly perch on the edge of the settee.

Erick enters the room balancing food in one hand, a bottle of Chianti and juice glasses in the other.

Occasionally, my recovering alcoholic grandmother will pitch a fit about my drinking and resort to breaking my stemware in protest.

Regardless of the fact that I'm not an alcoholic, her AA aphorisms occasionally get the best of her. We've reached an accord that involves drinking wine from simple juice glasses.

Thankfully, the wards and sigils Silas used to protect our new place from uninvited ghost pop-ins also allow us to have lovely wine and champagne glasses in the cupboards of our walk-up.

"Little help, Moon?"

"Right. Sorry. I smelled the garlic bread and then went catatonic."

Jumping from the settee, I grab the food while Erick opens the Chianti and pours us each a glass.

Grams floats from the closet, clucking her tongue, and I raise a warning finger in her direction. "I would advise you not to test me on an empty stomach, Isadora."

My hubby wisely leaves well enough alone and opens the containers of lasagna.

The first bite of that melted cheese, homemade sauce, and proprietary-recipe sausage, brings a broad smile to my face. "Mmm mm, good."

Erick, with a mouth as full as mine, nods in agreement.

The rest of our supper is silent, except for an occasional satisfied sigh.

"Are you going to try on the last gown, sweetie?"

Jumping into my role as afterlife interpreter, I share Ghost-ma's question with Erick and jerk a thumb in her general direction.

He glances over my shoulder and speaks to what he perceives as an empty space. "I absolutely respect your fashion sense, Isadora. But I guarantee you there's nothing in that closet that beats that little red number."

Grams' ghostly visage shuffles through a series of expressions before landing on satisfaction. She is clearly upset the fashion show is incomplete, but she's reveling in Erick's praise.

"It looks like your gown is all taken care of,

dear. Are you going to need any help with your hair tomorrow?"

"I doubt it, Grams. I've definitely perfected the French roll." Pausing for a quick swig of wine, I continue. "You're the one who taught me to wield a bobby pin with competence. If there's any problem, we've still got supplies in this bathroom."

She nods thoughtfully. "Let's pull a couple tendrils loose and bend those around the styling wand. I'm sure a few soft curls will add some romance to the look."

"Well, you're the expert, Grams."

She crosses her arms and grins broadly. "That I am."

Erick gathers the trash, glasses, and remaining Chianti. "We better call it a night. Sounds like a big day of prep tomorrow." He can barely hide his smirk.

"G'nite, Grams. I'll handle my hair and makeup over in the walk-up, and then I'll report to the sacred closet, all right?"

"That's fine, dear. What about Erick?"

Putting on my best Marilyn Monroe impression, I pass along the query. "Grams is asking about your outfit, darling."

His deep-blue eyes widen. "I have a tux." The words come out, but there's no commitment in the tone.

"Tell him I'll have to see it, dear. We can't have any subpar wardrobe items making an appearance at Cromwell Pearson's." She shakes her head in dismay. "Oh! Look at that, sweetie. I remembered Cromwell's name." Her wattage increases at least ten percent.

"Grams can't wait to see your outfit." My warm smile and drastic paraphrase will have to do. Erick is in no mood to deal with the ghost of fashion police.

Relief floods through him, and he heads out of the apartment.

Ghost-ma zooms after us, sputtering about creases and lapels.

Resorting to telepathic communication, I offer her a final word of warning. *Not today, Myrtle Isadora. We're respecting Erick's boundaries.*

"Reow." Can confirm.

Nice. For once, Pye is on my side.

Hold on! I didn't say anything out loud. Has that demon spawn of a cat been able to communicate telepathically this whole time?

I swear there's a feline snicker as the bookcase door slides closed behind me.

CHAPTER 6

THE AIR OF MYSTERY surrounding tonight's event definitely adds to the thrill.

Since I'm still tucked away in the luxurious bathroom attached to the primary suite on the third-floor walk-up, it's safe to admit Grams is right about feeling like I've finally arrived.

I never set out to be courted or accepted by Pin Cherry Harbor's upper crust, but the broke barista trapped inside the heiress feels vindicated. Checking my bobby pin placement in the mirror, I'd say this is the best French roll I've ever created. Each pin is carefully hidden, and the roll is smooth and even.

I don't have any natural ability with hair. Basically, I missed out on all the years when my mother might've passed along her tips and tricks. She always looked completely pulled together, despite our lack of disposable income.

The French roll was the first hairdo Grams taught me when I arrived in town. At that time, my hair was mostly a disaster. I'd lost a bet on a wild night out with friends and ended up with a cross between a long, fringy pixie and a strange bob. The mess was in large part due to chopping it off myself.

New and improved me resisted the temptation to cut my own hair for months on end. The additional length made today's job even easier. I'm not exactly sure how many tendrils Grams intended for me to pull loose and twist around my styling wand, but I've done what I can.

A final coat of gloss on my lips and one more layer of mascara do the trick.

Pulling the belt on my robe tight, I prepare for what awaits me in the enormous walk-in closet in my old apartment that I've nicknamed *Sex and the City* meets *Confessions of a Shopaholic*. As I tread down the final block of stairs, Erick looks up and whistles like a construction worker at a job site.

"You are working that robe, Moon."

"Put a cork in it, Harper. And clear a path. I have to get over to the closet and submit to my grandmother's wishes."

When I reach the last step, he grabs both ends of the terrycloth belt and pulls me close.

"Sure, but hear me out. We could ditch this robe—"

"Erick No Middle Name Harper! If you know what's good for you, you'll grab that tuxedo and fall in line behind me. You have no idea what kind of havoc an angry ghost can create. Get in formation, soldier."

He pops an official salute, grabs the garment bag holding his tuxedo, and marches behind me all the way to our destination.

CUT TO —

Erick passes muster without a single correction and leaves me floundering alone amongst elbow-length opera gloves, vats of jewelry, and varieties of shapewear I dare not mention.

Once my grandmother releases me from her clutches, I turn left and right in front of the full-length mirror and sigh with begrudging satisfaction.

Red is a lovely color on a fair-skinned girl with snow-white hair. The gorgeous diamond and ruby pendant that dangles on my décolletage is an heirloom piece my grandmother received from her fourth husband. The simple flake of diamond in the vintage wedding ring on my right hand pales in comparison.

However, the genuine love coursing around

that circle — both Odell Johnson's to my grandmother, the original owners, and now Erick's to me — makes up for any lack of ostentatious gems.

Wearing my wedding ring on the right hand was not a choice. There's an antique mood ring resting firmly on my left ring finger. It's not something I can technically remove. Once the ring and I reached a certain level of symbiosis, it had to remain in place. Not that its moodiness has changed. It sends me images at will. On a few occasions, I've been able to summon a little assistance, but it's nothing to be relied upon.

With a final tug at the dress, and a check of the ankle straps on my shiny red shoes, I'm free.

I wonder what Erick will think of this?

"He'll think you're a knockout, sweetie. And you absolutely are."

Pointing with a perturbed gesture toward my closed mouth, I know she receives the message.

Her shimmering shoulders attempt an innocent shrug.

Twiggy left early because of special dinner plans with her beau, Wayne. So I take advantage of the empty bookshop below and press the mother-of-pearl intercom button next to the secret door in the apartment. "I hope you're ready, Mr. Harper. Prepare to have your mind blown."

The hidden door slides open. I strut across the

Rare Books Loft, pausing at the top of the staircase. I'm happy to see my announcement was heeded. Erick stands at the bottom, mouth open, eyes wide, and one finger beckoning me to descend.

My cheeks turn as red as my dress while I carefully pick my way down the staircase.

He unhooks the chain, offers me a hand, and secures it behind me.

Adjusting his red bowtie, I gaze up and sigh. "When do you think the sleigh will get here?"

Erick shrugs and slips an arm around my waist. "Sunset is in five minutes." His eyes scan me from head to toe. "You're gonna need a jacket, or make that a full-length coat."

Grams swirls around us, smiling foolishly. "You two are the perfect couple. Absolutely dashing. Just dashing!"

"Grams thinks we look great."

Erick takes a bow and thanks my grandmother.

"Grams, I definitely need a coat. Any ideas?"

She spins rapidly, and as she slows her pace, a beautiful white faux fur, full-length coat appears out of thin air.

"How did you do that?"

"I'm learning how to take the occasional item from the physical plane — temporarily — and transport it to a new location. What do you think?"

My husband hesitantly plucks the coat from

midair and holds it while I slip my arms into the soft satin lining.

"I think it's a neat trick, Grams. But remember how we talked about you conserving your energy? Let's put any further antics on hold. All right?"

She crosses her arms, pushes out her bottom lip, and pouts. "Fine."

A chorus of jangling bells draws our attention to First Avenue.

Erick raises a finger. "I'll ask him to pull down the alley. I know you don't have your special key tucked under that little dress."

Once again, my cheeks flush with heat as he jogs toward the alleyway door to direct our transport.

Climbing into the sleigh is easier than I'd imagined. The driver folds down a set of two sturdy steps, and Erick is happy to offer his support as he boosts me into the shiny black sleigh.

The midnight-black Friesian stallions pulling the sleigh, whinny with anticipation as the driver snaps the reins. The clip-clopping of the horses' hooves is muffled by the snow cover, and the heater opposite our feet provides life-sustaining warmth.

I'd pictured the ride being as unpleasant as a winter trip in my mentor's 1908 Ford Model T, but this adventure is romance on steroids.

Erick warms my hands in his and gently kisses my cheek.

The snow twinkles like diamonds in the gloaming, and I lose all track of time.

When we pull up to the gates of the impressive winery, I feel as though I've been in a trance.

Châteauneuf-du-Nord.

Here goes nothing. I hope I don't embarrass Ghost-ma!

CHAPTER 7

Flickering torches line the drive, guiding us all the way to the grand entrance. The sleigh crunches to a halt in the snow. Two footmen silently approach, pull down the steps, and each takes one of my hands as I carefully descend.

Erick quickly moves in to support me down the potentially icy walkway, but, luckily, our host has seen to everything. The path has been salted and shoveled clean.

We pass by fire and ice as we proceed. Bright torches separate elaborate ice sculptures of the goddess of love — some towering above my head.

At the end of the walkway, stands an enormous arched wooden door opened by another member of staff. As we pass by, it's impossible not to notice the door's edge is thicker than the width of my hand. Impressive construction.

Entering the twinkling foyer, I gaze up at the high ceilings and a glittering chandelier, nearly walking right by the coat-check girl who's decked-out in feathery angel wings.

My helpful date takes my coat, passes it to the waiting woman, and pockets the claim ticket.

Curiosity gets the best of me. I have to ask. "Cupid?"

She shrugs. "No idea. Don't tell Mr. Pearson. I think we're all some different kinds of angels of love."

I chuckle and wink. It won't be a problem keeping her secret, since I have absolutely no idea who Mr. Pearson is.

"Mitzy Moon and Erick Harper! Birch County's new power couple, I see."

A rotund man with impeccably coiffed thick grey hair opens his arms wide as though we're his long-lost children.

He closes the distance, shakes Erick's hand first, then lifts my knuckles to his lips and offers a warm but definitely too-wet kiss to the back of my fingers.

I struggle mightily to hide my disgust. My grandmother's voice echoes in my head. "You catch more flies with honey."

Deep breath.

"Good evening, Mr. Pearson. Absolutely gorgeous venue. Lovely sleigh ride. Thank you so much for the invitation." I'm rambling.

He offers me a perfunctory smile and returns his attention to Erick.

"So glad you could come, Erick. When I heard you'd left the sheriff's department, I had to hear the full story for myself. Must be something big, to take a man like you away from his responsibilities."

Erick opens his mouth to answer, but another couple bursts through the arched doorway, and our host is off.

"Oh, I'm sure you'll excuse me. I must greet the guests. We'll chew the fat later." Once again, he never actually makes eye contact with me.

Pearson's booming voice fills the small space as he verbally accosts the next couple, and I'm grateful when Antoinette emerges from the shadows, gesturing for Erick and me to follow her.

She's practically unrecognizable. Her dark hair is scooped into an updo of loose curls, and her athletic shoulders are hidden beneath a shimmering silver gown. Plus, she's wearing lipstick.

"Let me get you guys into the tasting room for some appetizers." She gestures to the server carrying a tray of stemware and retrieves two glasses. She hands one to me first and then to Erick. "This is our latest sparkling Moscato. The grapes are from the vitis vinifera family, and were grown here. Processed, fermented, and bottled on site. One hundred percent Châteauneuf-du-Nord original. It will pair nicely with the charcuterie."

Erick and I each take a sip of the wine, and he nods his appreciation.

I take a page from one of my film school assignment movies, *Sideways*, and offer a bit more as I tilt the glass in the light. "Love the color. Rather buttery. And nice legs." Taking a deep inhale, I sip and swish. "The bouquet is somewhat floral, but there's a very subtle hint of oak on the tongue. Then peach . . . tobacco on the finish."

My date presses his lips together firmly, and my extra senses pick up on a suppressed snicker.

Nettie, on the other hand, takes me at my word. "Very good, Mitzy. I had no idea you had such an educated palate. Almost no one picks up on the tobacco in the finish. But that's exactly the note that got us the gold medal — twice. My father is going to be very impressed with you."

At this point in the evening, I can't even blame my next outburst on overindulgence in wine. It's simply what I do. "Really? Because he didn't seem to pay much attention to me when I got here. He only had eyes for Erick."

Nettie swallows hard, takes my glass, and beckons us farther into the shadows. "He's a man's man. Some might call him a chauvinist, or a cretin." She throws back the rest of my wine in an unexpected gulp.

My extra senses kick into full-on Spidey mode. "Hey, I'm sorry. I was only making a joke."

She snatches another Moscato from a passing tray and rolls her warm brown eyes. "I know. It's just a sensitive subject for me. I'm the oldest. My blood, sweat, and tears built this vineyard, and my father's going to hand it off to my younger brother. Because Napoleon is the oldest son." She throws one hand in the air and downs half of the fresh glass of sparkling wine.

I place a hand on her arm and attempt to send her some calming energy, as my mentor has offered me on so many previous occasions. "Seriously, forget about that. It's a celebration. You're the one who made all this possible, right? Not Napoleon."

She exhales loudly. "You know what? Leon doesn't want anything to do with this place. He went to university for physics. Then got his masters in more *physics*. I went to a viticulture program, and, through years of meticulous grafting, created my own original grape. But now, Leon is going to take over because he has a—"

Erick places a hand on Nettie's shoulder and squeezes. "Hey, cooler heads, okay? Remember on the field when you let your emotions get the better of you?"

Her gaze drifts to a faraway place, and I sense her remembering their days of high school football.

"Yeah, okay." She punches him playfully. "Still the QB, eh?"

"I'm not quarterbacking you, Nettie. I'm on your side."

Her shoulders relax, and she nods silently. "Yeah, I need to get a hold of myself. Tonight is not the night to have one of my legendary confrontations with papa. I'm supposed to give a speech. Possibly." She hands her wine glass to Erick without drinking the rest and saunters into the growing crowd.

My abilities pick up on a strange ache in her being. It's not the mutual admiration of one football player to another.

"Mr. Harper, is there something you're not telling me about Nettie?"

He sets her glass on a nearby high-top, draped in red and gold lamé, and gazes out at the crowd as he takes another sip of his wine. "Look, a 'photo op' booth. Let's get a pic, Moon."

My gaze takes in the grapevine archway, fairy lights, and a backdrop of — I'm assuming — their vineyards, ripe with grapes. "You have a two-minute reprieve."

We strike a dorky pose and tilt our heads together as the flash blinds us.

Erick grabs another glass of Moscato and scoops his arm around my waist. "Let's check out the appetizer buffet."

His effort to distract me is noble. "Let me see. It seems that a sheriff I once dated told me that avoidance of a question is a sure sign of guilt."

He spits a bit of his wine back into the glass and draws the attention of a few nearby connoisseurs.

Erick waves a hand and pats his chest. "Went down the wrong pipe. It's delicious. That was all me."

Hooking my arm through his elbow, I drag him closer to the charcuterie and the scent of Camembert and soppressata. "What aren't you telling me, Ricky?"

"If you were anyone but *you* . . . Since you'll figure it out anyway, I'll save us both some time. I took Nettie to prom."

My mouth opens, but no words fall out.

He shakes his head and attempts to wave off whatever he thinks is coming. "No. It's not like that. She's, you know . . . she doesn't like guys. But in high school, she wasn't ready to make that public knowledge. Nettie wanted to go to prom, and I wanted to avoid the obligation of going with some mean-girl cheerleader, just to check all the social boxes."

"So, you were simply helping out a teammate. You and Nettie weren't an item?"

His laughter is genuine. "Not even close. In fact, we—"

"Well, if it isn't the Prom King?"

This man bears little resemblance to Cromwell Pearson. Instead, he shares Nettie's shiny black hair, but his eyes are a wily brown rather than warm. He tosses an arm around Erick's shoulder and gives a pat as he laughs loudly.

"Napoleon Pearson. I knew you'd be here, but— Man, you haven't changed a bit. This wine must be bottled straight from the fountain of youth."

Napoleon laughs heartily, but his eyes immediately wander to my cleavage.

"If it isn't the delicious Mitzy Moon. I've heard quite a lot about you from Pin Cherry's movers and shakers." He arches one dark eyebrow as he reaches toward me.

Switching my wineglass to my right hand, I easily avoid shaking his proffered limb. "I prefer the adjective intelligent. It's less demeaning and objectifying. Would you not agree?" Throwing out the phrasing so often used by my mentor creates exactly the right amount of confusion on Napoleon's lecherous face.

A striking redhead in a white Givenchy evening gown, adorned with feathers, grabs Leon's arm. "Remember me?" Once she commandeers her husband, her fiery gaze falls on me.

If looks could kill.

I struggle to smile.

Erick tosses me a sympathetic look, but, ever the peacemaker, quickly changes the topic. "Nettie mentioned you'd married a wonderful woman. Is this your better half?"

That line of questioning does the trick. Within seconds, Leon is tripping over himself trying to make his wife sound like a goddess descended to earth, leaving an easy gap for me to slip away and fill a plate with snacks.

As I take a large bite of onion and apricot tartlet, a hush falls over the crowd. Our stout host has taken center stage. Cromwell's deep voice resonates. "Honored guests, my beautiful wife, Aurélie."

CHAPTER 8

Externally, he seems proud of the woman who struts into the room, but I have the advantage of several senses not gifted to the average human. There's an undercurrent of distrust, dislike, and a soupçon of hatred that's palpable to my extra abilities.

The children, at least the two I've met, definitely get their refined looks from their elegant, dark-haired mother.

Aurélie makes a shallow curtsy, and her melodic French voice floats through the room like the tender notes of a heartfelt aria. "*Bienvenue à tous*. Welcome, everyone. We are so pleased to have you with us this evening. My husband has selected some of our finest wines, and I endeavored to pair them with scrumptious food. It is our hope that your palate will be both excited and sated."

Cromwell strides toward her and draws the attention back to himself. "Follow me to the great hall." He walks toward an archway decorated with grapevines and tiny lights.

We pass into a massive entertaining hall where one entire wall is decorated with stacked barrel ends. "Find your name card and join me at the table."

He moves to the head of the table while others mill around, searching for their name cards.

Our Orson-Welles-sized host settles into his enormous chair and reaches for his wineglass, eager to resume holding court.

However, all eyes turn toward the rear archway as a small group, led by a man who is the spitting image of Aurélie, enters boisterously. Elegant cheekbones, dark swept bangs, and a penetrating gaze. This must be the youngest brother, whom I've not yet met.

He gestures to his entourage. "May I introduce our guests . . ."

At that moment, I pull off a little sleight-of-hand at the long supper table and swap Erick's card with Leon's. There's absolutely no way I'm sitting next to that leering physicist for an entire evening.

Tucking my arm through Erick's elbow, I tug him toward the table.

He tilts his head and smiles. "What's your hurry?"

"We need to sit down. I may or may not have fiddled with the name cards."

Once again, he nearly chokes on his wine.

Quickly taking our seats, it pleases me greatly to see the utter disappointment on Leon's face when he approaches what he thought was his chair.

The dashing young fellow at the far end of the great hall finishes introducing his laughing entourage and calls for libations.

Cromwell Pearson rises from his chair and bellows, "Emmanuel! So good of you to join us."

Emmanuel takes a sarcastic bow. "I wouldn't miss it for the world, dear Father. Our guests enjoyed the private tour of the wine cellar and were especially impressed with your 1858 Porto Valriz."

Fury rages behind Cromwell's carefully controlled faceplate. Emmanuel must've played fast and loose with a rare specimen. "Only a fool wouldn't be impressed by the collection I've amassed, son. Now, I've asked everyone to take their seats. Sooner rather than later."

Emmanuel mumbles under his breath, but my extrasensory perception provides easy auditory access. He snarls, "I'd never dream of disappointing you, old man."

The great hall has a massive arched ceiling

dotted with shimmering chandeliers. The sparkling light glimmers off the gold chargers placed in front of each of the twenty chairs on either side of an extraordinarily long table. Cromwell is, of course, at the head of the table, seated in a massive captain's chair. Shockingly, Aurélie has earned a place at the foot of the table, but, not that surprisingly, in a much smaller chair.

When the guests have settled into their assigned seating, a parade of servers pours from what must be the kitchen and down either side of the table. Footed crystal salad bowls are placed on each charger.

Once again, the blunderbuss that is Cromwell Pearson gets to his feet and man-splains this course to us.

"Before you, I have placed artisanal applewood-smoked bacon on a bed of radicchio and rocket. The bleu cheese is smoked on-site, and the candied walnuts are the chef's secret recipe. A drizzle of pomegranate balsamic is the only dressing required for this scrumptious first course. This will be paired with our dry Riesling, which has been a gold medal winner three years running." He lifts his crystal wineglass. "Cheers."

The guests all dutifully echo his toast, drink the wine, moan in mostly feigned ecstasy, and dig into their salads.

Erick leans toward me and whispers, "So you didn't want to spend the evening next to Leon?"

I shoot him a "don't test me" stare and shake my head. He grins knowingly and takes a huge bite of his schmancy salad.

As we finish our first course, servers seem to fall out of the woodwork to remove our empty bowls and refill our water goblets. Empty wineglasses are removed. Heaven knows we don't want to contaminate the next tasting with the dregs of our thrice-gold dry Riesling.

Rows of servers reemerge and swap the gilded chargers for our entrées in one smooth motion. Like a choreographed drill team, when those with full hands peel away from the table, they are quickly replaced by a fresh bastion of servers bearing our next wine pairing.

"A rare treat this evening, friends. I own a cattle ranch, and we've been experimenting with bourbon-fed beef. Our cattle enjoy ten gallons of bourbon silage per day — still warm from the distillery when it hits the trough. The tenderloins served by Chef this evening were expertly carved by a butcher this morning."

The thought makes me gag, and it's only Erick's tight grip on my knee that keeps me from depositing my award-winning dry Riesling on the fancy tablecloth.

"The side of dauphinoise potatoes is meant as a palate cleanser." He glances toward the foot of the table with disdain. Clearly the potatoes were not his idea and are beneath his standards. Apparently, he and Aurélie don't see eye to eye on party planning.

"Please note, the Pinot Noir I've selected, which was a Best Wine of 2022, will bring out the rich cherry and honey subtleties in your main course. Enjoy!"

Once again, the guests diligently raise their glasses, inhale deeply, and take the obligatory sip. Some of the better actors in the group nearly swoon at the first taste of the legendary Pinot Noir.

I, on the other hand, dive directly into my potatoes and refuse to have anything to do with the unsettling beef.

Erick deftly moves my tenderloins to his plate and has no problem devouring a second portion.

The serving sizes are small and exquisitely plated. Very French. It doesn't take long for the guests to finish their main course.

With a delicate swirl of her dignified hand, Aurélie waves in the string quartet while the servers clear all the dinner plates, flatware, and stemware in a reset for the dessert course.

Cromwell rises, and, rather than politely asking the string quartet to pause, he simply shouts over them. "In a moment, you will experience the crème brûlée cheesecake. Select coffee or tea with this course, which I'm only serving at my wife's request." He gives her a look that says, "I tolerate your existence."

She smiles back in a way that screams, "I'd love to kill you in your sleep."

Yikes. This family has serious problems.

"The true dessert will be served after this fluff course. I will retrieve a cask of my world-famous tawny port. Each of you will be treated to a tasting directly from the barrel. After which we will all proceed to the bottling room, where you will be able to see this vintage bottled tonight. It will be forty years before the precious liquid is available for sale."

Ooohs, aaahs, and gasps abound. It amazes me how he takes credit for every little thing, regardless of the fact he's actually done nothing.

He smiles with an air of superiority that turns my stomach. "The best is yet to come. After the bottling, please return to the tasting room, where you will have the distinct pleasure of sampling our first public offering of a forty-year-aged tawny port."

Light applause.

Cromwell nods dismissively. "My grandfather handpicked these grapes, and my father transferred that vintage from the barrels to the bottles forty years ago." There's a dramatic pause, and he presses two thick fingers to his mouth in a performance of emotion. "Knowing he would not live to taste his own extraordinary creation. Tonight, his legacy will live on. This is sure to be our next gold-medal-winning offering."

Raucous applause breaks out, and a few of the obsessed get to their feet.

"Our winemaker Philippe will retrieve the barrel, but I assure you the glory that resides within is entirely due to the Pearson expertise."

From the wings, I hear an angry Frenchman curse the fat American blowhard.

"Philippe? Where are you, boy? Your moment has come."

I'd say there are at least one hundred and fifty ways to be inconsiderate, and Cromwell Pearson knows all of them.

Philippe, an angular face framed by salt-and-pepper hair, emerges from the shadows and shares a dangerous look with Aurélie.

He offers a curt nod to Mr. Pearson and disappears deeper into the winery. Moments later, Philippe rushes back into the room and whispers frantically in Pearson's ear.

"Fix it, you idiot Frog. What do I pay you for?"

"I tried. My key isn't—"

"As usual, I have to do everything myself!" The

corpulent Cromwell storms off with Philippe at his heels like a dog.

Those of us left at the table exchange uncomfortable glances as Aurélie motions to the string quartet to kick into a new song.

The cello thrums through a solo, and the guests breathe a sigh of relief.

From the depths of Châteauneuf-du-Nord—

An earsplitting crash followed by a strangled scream seems to stop time.

CHAPTER 9

THE FIRST PERSON out of their chair is former sheriff Erick Harper. He sprints toward the commotion, and I follow as quickly as I'm able in four-inch heels!

Just ahead of me, Nettie shouts to Erick. "It came from the fermentation room!"

She pushes open the door, stops cold, and screams in blood-curdling horror.

Erick grips her arm and pulls her out of the room as he calmly gives her instructions.

"Nettie, look at me. I need you to call 911. Tell them to send an ambulance, the paramedics, and a fire truck. Repeat it back to me."

Her breathing is rapid, and I feel terror rolling off her in waves. She looks at her old teammate and repeats the instructions with precision. Erick could've easily placed the call himself, but he's giving her a task to distract her from whatever awful thing lurks behind that door.

Nettie pulls her phone from a nifty pocket in her dress and steps to the side. I follow Erick into the fermentation room and immediately wish I hadn't.

The tableau that greets me is too macabre to describe. My tummy swirls in protest.

The room is lined with rows of heavy steel pallet racks curved at each level to receive giant casks of wine. And by giant, I'm not kidding around. These are bigger than any fifty-five-gallon drums I've ever seen. The massive wooden barrels are cradled three high, row upon row, the length of the room.

The thing that's out of place is the collapsed pallet rack missing its top barrel — and what remains of Mr. Pearson lying beneath it.

To the right of the gruesome discovery lies Philippe. He must've been standing close enough to Cromwell to be injured severely by the falling cask, but not killed.

Philippe is writhing in pain and bleeding profusely from a compound fracture in his right leg.

I'm no medic, but there's a chance the technique Silas fortuitously taught me could help this man.

Swallowing hard and focusing on Philippe's face, I crouch next to the moaning winemaker and extend my left hand toward his— I can't mention the injury, or I'll lose my entire Valentine's gala meal.

Without looking directly at the horrible break, I recite the magic hand mantra and hover my left hand as steadily as possible over the wounded leg.

Philippe's moaning instantly ceases. He gazes up with shock swimming in his eyes. "Qu'est-ce que c'est? You are a sorceress?"

"It's nothing. I grew up in Sedona. Probably some energy work I picked up. Just lie back and try to slow your breathing. Paramedics will be here soon." His fear is palpable, but I have to push it away and hold my focus.

Erick has employed Nettie and Leon to cordon off the area.

A hysterical cry echoes outside the door. Oddly, Aurélie is late to the party.

"*Mon cœur*! Let me see my husband!"

Erick's calming voice addresses the freshly minted widow. "Mrs. Pearson, there's been a terrible accident. First responders are on their way, but I'm afraid Mr. Pearson has died in a— You don't want to see him like this. I'm so sorry."

Her wailing penetrates the closed door of the fermentation room, but my abilities aren't available to verify its authenticity. I have to stay focused on the task at hand because if my attention wanders for even a moment, Philippe begins to moan.

The door swings open.

"Well, if it isn't our local corpse magnet." The short, squat sheriff rocks back and forth in all her polyester glory. "Moon, get away from that man. I don't need you contaminating my crime scene."

Oh, goody. Paulsen responded. I don't remember Erick mentioning anything about calling the sheriff. Before I can slap her with a dose of my signature snark, Philippe hurries to my defense. "*S'il vous plaît*, Sheriff, let her stay. She's helping. The pain is too much. Please!"

Paulsen's right hand firmly grips the handle of her holstered gun, and she mumbles her objection before offering a cursory nod.

Deputies Johnson and Gilbert herd the guests back to the great hall. I'm sure Paulsen has them taking statements.

Erick returns with the paramedics and, much to Philippe's disappointment, I step back. As soon as I remove my hovering hand from his injury, the pain returns and the blood flows.

One of the paramedics looks at me suspiciously, while the other tends to the wound.

My husband pulls me aside, and my gaze drags

across the unpleasant and unforgettable scene under the barrel.

"Mitzy. Do you see that?" His voice is barely a whisper, and he subtly gestures to the steel pallet rack.

Taking a deep breath, I struggle to ignore the disaster on the floor and focus on the area Erick indicated.

"That looks like—"

He finishes my sentence. "Someone sawed partway through the metal. This was no accident." Erick surreptitiously snaps a few "just in case" pics on his phone.

I'm glad one of us has their wits about them. My stomach is still flip-flopping like a fish out of water.

Paramedics load Philippe onto a gurney and roll him out of the fermentation room. Erick tugs me along in their wake.

"You give your statements to the deputies like everyone else, Harper." Paulsen sucks air between her teeth and juts her chin in our general direction.

Now that she's officially won an election and is the actual sheriff and not the interim sheriff, there's literally no living with her.

Erick nods politely. "You got it, Sheriff." I open my mouth to protest, but he propels me toward the great hall.

En route, the meal I so carefully kept down while I was helping Philippe demands an encore.

Glancing at Erick, I groan, cover my mouth with one hand, and dart into the "Mademoiselle's."

After freeing my gala grub, I'm in desperate need of a freshen-up.

The mirror reflects my paltry efforts.

Yikes! All the alchemy in the world isn't going to save this dress.

Grams is never going to forgive me for ruining her couture, but she'll be relieved to know the blood on the gown isn't mine. Actually, that makes two of us. I hope Philippe will pull through.

When I return to the table, Erick slips an arm around me. "You okay, Moon?"

I lean into his embrace and whisper, "Is it wrong to say I could sure use a glass of wine?" He sputters and eventually laughs. "You and your dark humor. I'll see what I can do."

He steps out of the room and returns with a healthy pour of blessed Pinot Noir.

"Guess who's back there running the kitchen?"

I accept the wine, take a steadying gulp, and shrug my indifference.

"Remember that ultra-fancy boutique restaurant in Grand Falls where — I'm not going to say his name — took you, and you tripped on the stairs and twisted your ankle?"

One more glug of wine and its calming warmth is spreading. "Let's see, would that be the first time I met your mother? The first time I heard her call you Ricky?"

He blushes. "That's the time. Did I ever tell you how jealous I was that night?"

"You did not. But it should soothe your wound to know that it was not a great evening. That slimeball chef tried to consume my fingers as an appetizer. And, as you know, my date turned out to be a super-controlling dark sorcerer."

"Yeah, I remember that part." Erick shakes his head and exhales loudly.

He pulls me close and kisses the top of my head. Deputy Gilbert sees us waiting and hurries over. "Hey, I'll take your statements real quick and you guys can get out of here."

"Thanks, Gilbert."

"Any time."

We tell him what little we know, and I attempt to give him the location of everyone at the table at the time of the crash. However, the buzz of the Pinot Noir is officially interfering with my ability to access any psychic replay, and my efforts are lackluster.

"Hey, if I think of anything else, I'll call the station." My eyes glaze over as I shrug.

He makes a note on his pad. "Thanks. You guys are free to go."

Erick pauses to offer Nettie his condolences and apologizes that we weren't able to conduct the search of the premises for which we'd been hired.

"Hey, I still need you guys on the job. I don't think it was an accident." Several strands of her dark hair have come loose from her hairdo, and streaks of sweat create rivulets in her makeup.

Erick plays his cards close to the vest and doesn't tell her what we saw on the pallet rack. "No problem. We'll be back in the morning to conduct a thorough investigation. If there's any way you can make sure absolutely no one goes into that fermentation room after the medical examiner — finishes her collection — that would be great."

She nods. "Emmanuel and Deputy Johnson are friends." Her voice cracks, and she blinks back tears. "We'll pay him to stay here tonight and watch the crime scene."

"Thanks, Nettie." He gives her shoulder a comforting pat.

As we exit the great hall, Aurélie storms in spewing angry French phrases at her daughter. Nettie turns to fend her off, going toe-to-toe with the foreign-language argument.

Erick exhales and scoops an arm around me.

"Nettie always cursed in French when she got upset during a game. I had no idea she was fluent."

He retrieves my coat and tips the smiling jacket angel.

"Did you know her mother was French?" Outside the temperature has dropped, and the flickering torches are doing very little to warm my frosty toes.

A sleigh pulls up, and the footmen help me in.

"I wasn't tight with Nettie outside of school, and I never came to their house. Nettie talked about her mom and her uncle Philippe meeting Cromwell ages ago in France. I always assumed the French ancestry, because of the name of the winery, but I'd never met the woman until tonight."

"Philippe is Aurélie's brother? Cromwell treated him like dirt." I arch an eyebrow and purse my lips. "Maybe we should pay him a visit at the hospital before we head back to the winery tomorrow."

Erick brushes his cold lips against my cheek. "Harper and Moon are on the case."

CHAPTER 10

Back in Pin Cherry proper, Erick practically carries me from the sleigh as he bundles me into the walk-up.

The scene that greets us triggers Erick's lawman instincts. He shields me with his body and pulls me into a crouch.

Trash is strewn all over the kitchen and dining room.

"Was the door locked?"

He nods and holds a finger to his lips.

Reaching out with all my senses, I confirm we're safe. "There's no one here." However, I discover the energy of a smug feline in the darkness. "Pye! Did you do this?"

"Re-oow." A tolerant greeting.

Erick pulls me to my feet. "What did he say?"

It's adorable that he believes the cat can and does talk to me. "He's avoiding the question, but I can sense the guilt twitching his whiskers." Sigh. "I'll clean it up."

"Nope. Straight to bed for you, young lady." His false bravado includes taking my coat and hanging it in the entry closet.

Rubbing the crimson-dark patch of dried blood on my dress, I shake my head in silence.

"How about I help you out of that dress, toss it in a trashcan along with the rest of this mess, and get you in a hot shower?" His features are pinched with concern, and his soft gaze sends ripples of love in my direction, but I can't accept this help right now.

"I have to go talk to Grams. We need to set up the murder wall, and I—"

Tears trickle down my cheeks, and Erick scoops me into his powerful arms. "You don't have to do anything, Moon. You held it together like a pro back there. I don't know what you were doing for Philippe, but you helped him hang on until the paramedics arrived. I've seen trained soldiers in battle crack under less pressure. You need to rest."

Pyewacket circles around us.

"It's called Magic Hand. Silas taught me how to—"

A soft, whispered knock, like wire brushes on a snare drum, interrupts my speech.

"Grams? Grams, is that you?"

"It's me, sweetie. You know I can't get past the wards Silas put up."

I stuff a flash of guilt and pull myself from Erick's loving embrace. Hurrying to the door separating our walk-up from the bookshop, I throw it open and choke on my words as a fresh batch of tears spills from my eyes.

"Sweetie! You're crying!"

Grams swoops in to comfort me, but stops as though her ghostly aura has hit a brick wall.

"Are you stuck? I opened the door. You're welcome to come in."

Her ring-ensconced fist plants on her curvy hip. "Is that blood? You got blood on my vintage couture!"

Her ire is exactly the catalyst I need to snap out of the doldrums. "I would think the first question out of your mouth would be, 'Is that your blood, most precious granddaughter?'"

Guilt and shame turn her silver glow to muddy brown. "Oh, sweetie! Are you hurt? What was I thinking? Tell Erick to call a doctor."

Rubbing my hands over my face, I exhale loudly and grip the door handle for support. "It's not my blood, Isadora. But there was a murder at the event of the season." A wry smile curves my mouth. "The murder of the season, if you will."

The remaining color drains from her apparition and she pantomimes her shock like an old Hollywood talkie flick. Her shimmering mouth forms a silent "who."

"It was Cromwell Pearson."

"Are you sure?"

My knees feel weak, and a convulsive shiver grips my entire body.

Rushing toward the glowing embers in the fireplace, I call out to Erick. "Grams is asking if I'm sure Cromwell is dead. Can you fill in the details for her and Pyewacket? I'm freezing."

He walks toward me, grabbing the chenille throw from the back of the couch. Once he's wrapped me, rubbed my shoulders somewhat aggressively, stoked the fire, and kissed the top of my head, he brings the rest of the Scooby Gang up to speed.

Despite his best efforts, Grams continues to toss questions my way.

I don't want the job of afterlife interpreter right now, but if I don't deliver, she'll demand 3 x 5 cards and a pen.

"Hold on a sec. Grams wants to hear about the menu first." Since the fare has nothing to do with the deadly disaster, I field the food- and décor-related questions, and, once the film-school dropout in me has handled the mise-en-scène, I toss it back to Erick. "All right, she's ready for the — you know."

He delicately relays the horror of Cromwell's death, and I shift my focus to the flickering firelight.

The mood ring on my left hand burns with its own heat, and I gaze into the smoky cabochon to see what message awaits.

Nettie running toward us — FROM the direction of the fermentation room.

Curious. I'll mention it tomorrow. Tonight, I can't take anymore sleuthing.

I know, I'm as shocked as you.

Grams swirls aimlessly as Erick wraps up his tale. "So, we'll have to wait for confirmation from the ME, but Cromwell is the one who walked out of the great hall with Philippe, and he was the only one missing after the incident. Right, Mitzy?"

My gaze slides toward him, but no words come out.

Erick glances over his shoulder at me. "Cromwell was the only one missing after the incident, right?"

Inhaling deeply just to settle my nerves, I risk a quick mental replay.

"Yeah. Nettie was ahead of us, Aurélie was late, and Leon helped— Wait, what am I saying? It was him. I have full psychic confirmation that it was

Cromwell Pearson under the—" Pressing a hand to my mouth, I shake the images away.

Grams floats closer, fidgets with the wedding ring on her left pointer finger, and attempts a smile. "You'll take the dress to the dry cleaner first thing tomorrow, won't you?"

"Grams! Stop worrying about the dress. But yes, I'll take it to the dry cleaner first thing in the morning, and maybe Tan— I mean, Pilar — can get the stain out."

Erick has taken on the task of drop-offs and pickups at the dry cleaner since we opened our new office. I haven't actually set foot in the place since Tanya's murder — but that's another story.

Erick scans the room. "Isadora? I'm assuming you're still here. I need to get Mitzy in the shower and tucked into bed. She's been through it tonight. If I remember correctly, it takes a lot of her personal energy to do these alchemical workings Silas teaches her. She had to use something called a magic hand on Philippe for quite a while."

Grams swoons over Erick's heartfelt concern for me. I'm too weak to pass that along.

He continues. "Can I leave the murder wall set up to you and Pyewacket?"

Ghost-ma silently pops a salute while Pyewacket offers verbal confirmation. "RE-OW!" Game on!

"I'll take that as a 'yes' for the group." Erick sees Pyewacket out. Thankfully, Grams follows, and then he supports me up to the en suite on the third floor.

Grabbing two fresh towels, he turns on the space heater in the bathroom.

I robotically undress and step into the shower. The steam fogs the glass, and, as Erick quietly exits, I allow myself to escape into the memory of my first Valentine's Day in Pin Cherry Harbor. Just the good parts.

Sure there was a murder. Yes, I solved it. However, the highlight of that year's Cupid-based celebration was a heart-melting homemade Valentine from Sheriff Erick Harper, with a special message on the back.

Dear Mitzy,

You're the most fascinating (and infuriating) woman I've ever met. I'm glad you came to Pin Cherry, and I'm glad you're going to stay. You're going to stay, right? Erick.

I stayed. Oh, how glad I am that I did. Mmhmm. I've never made a better decision in my entire life.

The eucalyptus bath products replace the scent

of hairspray and crime-scene debris. When I finally reach for the faucet and twist the flow of water to a stop, I feel re-energized on the inside and refreshed on the outside.

Stepping out of the shower, I wrap a thick towel around my head and a second around my person. Maybe I do have the energy to set up the murder wall?

When I walk from the bathroom into the primary suite, the loud crackle of a roaring fire greets me.

The firelight twinkles in Erick's eyes as he flips back the thick down comforter and pats a spot next to him on the soft-as-silk bamboo sheets.

The muscles in his arms flex as he takes my hand and pulls me close. And there's more than firelight glinting in his eyes when he tosses one of my towels to the floor.

CHAPTER 11

THE BLEAK FEBRUARY SUN leaking around the edges of our blackout blinds comes as no surprise. I've been lying awake in bed for hours. The events of yesterday's gala make little sense and refuse to let me rest. Maybe it was the overstimulation of such an extravagant event or the overindulgence in wine, but I can't make heads or tails of the staged accident.

Next to me, my husband sleeps like a bear in hibernation.

My inner bad girl wants to nudge him sharply with a foot and force him to join my insomnia. However, he almost always wakes up before me and makes sure there's a steaming pot of coffee waiting. Now's my chance to return the favor.

Extracting myself from our cozy bed as quietly

as possible, I tuck my feet into Christmas unicorn slippers and pad down to the first floor.

Erick loves the convenience of our top-of-the-line coffeemaker. I, on the other hand, prefer the intensity of a handcrafted cup of java.

As I pour boiling water into the bottom section of the espresso contraption, tamp the grounds tightly into the small funnel-y bit, and twist on the top to marry the two halves, it's hard not to reminisce about my days as a broke barista.

While I wait for the brew to bubble on the stove, I slip into my memories.

As a coffee *artiste*, I may have been less than thrilled with the hours, insulted by the pay, and generally not in the mood to chitchat with customers, but oh, how I loved the free caffeine!

Arriving late for a shift and wasting additional time savoring a complimentary cup of black gold with not-sour half-and-half — that I also didn't have to purchase — has to be one of the most divine experiences of my forlorn orphan years.

I assumed I'd always be an orphan. Losing my mother when I was eleven, fighting my way through the foster system for almost six years, and coming out the other side of the school of hard knocks used to be my badge of honor.

Until Silas Willoughby came knocking on my door, my mother — when she wasn't calling me

Mippity Bippity Boo — was the only one who had called me Mizithra. It happens to be the name of a Greek cheese, and also the thing that brought her and my one-night-stand father together over twenty-five years ago.

Theirs had been a classic "meet cute." She was shopping at some over-priced hipster grocery store when my rumored-to-be irresistible father had reached for the same ball of mizithra cheese that my mom had grabbed. Their hands touched. Their eyes met. Cut to her apartment. Their naughty places touched. He never called. She kept the baby and her secret.

Maybe she named me after the cheese in some strange hope that he would return and they would share a laugh. That never happened during her lifetime. In fact, she never spoke of him. I came to believe he'd died. It was the only explanation a fatherless girl could accept.

Now that I call Pin Cherry Harbor my home, acts of philanthropy and the blessings of my found family exceed my wildest expectations. I mean, it was a bit of a gut punch to find out my biological father was alive and well. He told me about a time he'd returned to Arizona and looked up Coraline, only to discover her having ice cream with a child he knew instantly to be his offspring — it's this darn snow-white hair. His life was a mess, and, at that time, he walked away thinking I'd turn out just fine with a mother like Cora. He had no idea my mother wouldn't make it past my eleventh birthday. However, the grown-up part of me understands he truly believed I would be better off with her.

I agree with him on that last part. I was better off with her — when she was alive.

Coraline Moon was amazing. Worked multiple jobs, kept me clothed and fed, and added a little magic to my life every day. She read me wonderful stories, built blanket forts, and never talked down to me.

Meanwhile, my bio dad, Jacob Duncan, was rotting in a prison cell for crimes he mostly didn't commit. Clearing his name of a false murder charge became the catalyst for this whole amateur snooping gig.

I respect Erick's reasons for legitimizing things with the private investigation company, but part of me still misses the days of shooting from the hip and figuring it out later.

The telltale "end of cycle" burble of the espresso maker pulls me from my reverie.

Filling our largest mug with a generous portion of go-go juice, I add just the right amount of cream and shuffle to my old apartment.

"Grams?"

Pyewacket cracks a sleepy eyelid and fixes his golden orb on my mug of coffee.

"Come on, son. Don't look at me like that. I'll pour you a bowl of your favorite sugary children's cereal as soon as this caffeine kicks in."

He offers a nonchalant stretch, rolls away from me, and fails to rise from the antique four-poster bed he now claims as his own.

Fine by me. Turning my attention to the murder wall, I'm impressed by the progress Grams made. There are 3 x 5 cards for each of the Pearson family members, as well as Philippe, Aurélie's brother.

There's a long hunk of green yarn dangling from a single tack. I can hardly blame her for abandoning that task. Everyone is connected to everyone else. Winding green yarn hither and yon seems like a waste of energy, and I did ask her to conserve.

The rolling corkboard, which Twiggy insists we use, is an adequate device for visualizing the case.

If it were up to me, I'd simply tack things onto the walls, but I've been warned more than once that any damage to the original lath and plaster will result in severe consequences.

No idea what those might be, but I need Twiggy more than she needs me, so I don't push.

Angling the board toward the settee, I recline and slowly sip my coffee

I can't imagine anyone in the family killing Cromwell. Sure, Philippe seemed to dislike the man, but he would have nothing to gain.

Nettie may have been upset that her father refused to pass the winery down to her, but killing him wouldn't change that. Leon would still inherit.

Speaking of Leon, he may be a sleazy lecher, but he has less to gain than anyone else. He already stands to inherit everything. Killing his father wouldn't change the outcome for him one iota.

The youngest, Emmanuel, seems full of himself and rebellious, but not dangerous.

Catching a movement out of the corner of my eye, it warms my heart when Pyewacket slinks across the room and silently leaps onto the settee.

He drapes himself over my lap and allows me the privilege of scratching his broad tan head.

A low rumble thrums through his chest, and the weight of him comforts my inner anxiousness.

"What do you think, Pye? Got a new case here, and you haven't given me a single clue. Are you retiring from the sleuthing business?"

His black-tufted ears twitch sharply. "Ree-OW!" A warning punctuated by a threat.

"All right. All right. You gave me a receipt for online shopping. I didn't realize that was a clue. No need to be feisty."

Retrieving the slip of paper from the closet, I

tack it to the board and point. "Happy now, you furry demon spawn?"

"Re-ow." Thank you.

"We're gonna head over to the hospital and talk to Philippe. Maybe he saw something that will point us in the right direction. Meanwhile, use whatever super powers you possess, Robin Pyewacket Goodfellow, and see what you can dig up for me. Deal?"

"Reow." Can confirm.

An ethereal whistle, followed by pops and snaps of electricity, precedes the appearance of Ghost-ma.

"Oh, Mitzy. I never expected to see you up and around so early."

"Ha ha." Taking another sip of my java, I savor the life-giving liquid and gesture toward the rolling corkboard. "You did a great job on the murder wall, Grams. Any insight into our current case?"

"I can't say, dear. I wasn't a friend of the Pearsons. We bumped elbows at various social events, but Aurélie and I weren't what you would call close."

"Understood. Back in the day, I hung out in bars with plenty of folks I wouldn't invite into my apartment. And my apartment was a real piece of—"

"Mitzy!"

"What? I was going to say, 'archeological wonderment.'"

Grams laughs until she ghost snorts. "You're such a hoot."

"Anyway, I suppose you wouldn't have much need for favors from winemakers, seeing that you were a recovering alcoholic."

Her perfectly drawn eyebrows arch sharply. "Nonsense! You forget I raised a fortune for charities in this town. Despite my bumpy history with alcohol, I'm forced to admit that it's more than a social lubricant. It has a way of loosening many a purse string." She chuckles wickedly, and, for a split second, flames from another dimension flicker in the center of her glowing irises.

"Myrtle Isadora! You were quite the scheming socialite."

She flashes her eyebrows in my general direction, and a smug grin graces her flawless face.

"RE-ow." Feed me.

"Duty calls, Grams. I need to tend to his royal furriness and head over to the walk-up. I'll be back to update you when we return from the hospital."

She smiles warmly. "Give my best to Philippe."

"You can be sure I won—" Turning as the bookcase door slides open, I tilt my head in confusion. "You said you weren't friends with Aurélie. But you knew her brother?"

Grams shrugs her designer-gown-clad shoulders and avoids my gaze.

"Oh, I see. A *special friend*, perhaps? I keep forgetting we traced my tramp gene directly back to you."

As the door slides closed behind me, I hear her utter a barely indignant, "Well, I never!"

CHAPTER 12

ERICK

The Birch County Regional Medical Center is the beating heart of our county. Its modern architecture and high-tech upgrades seem out of place in the little town I've called home my entire life. Mitzy is right when she jokes that it's the town that tech forgot.

The meager local hospital that previously stood on this site served a quarter of the patients this new facility can manage. When my ma, Gracie Harper, went into labor over thirty-one years ago, she would've called her physician and met him in a crowded facility that handled everything from emergencies to sports physicals for athletes at the high school.

I've been to this new hospital, in my capacity as sheriff, more times than I can count. Checking up on wounded deputies, questioning suspects who injured themselves during their various crimes, or taking statements from frightened victims. No matter the reason, the front desk staff and nurses have always been kind and accommodating.

Even though I no longer wear the badge, the goodwill I built up over the years still carries weight within these walls.

As Mitzy and I approach the front desk, the grey-haired nurse handing coffee to the receptionist turns and smiles. “I knew you’d be in this morning, Mr. Harper. Might not be county sheriff, but I knew a case like this would grab your attention.”

After a quick glance at her name tag, I reply, “Thanks, Tammy. You’re right, as usual. Could you point us in the direction of Philippe Moueix’s room?”

She smiles warmly and offers a welcoming gesture. “Follow me. I’m headed up to the third floor right now.”

Beside me, Mitzy tucks her arm through my elbow as we enter the elevator and whispers, “Nice French, Harper. Mooh-ICKS.” She giggles.

Tammy points down the hallway when we exit. “Second room on the left. He hasn’t had any other visitors.”

I didn’t ask, but I’ll make a note of it. “Thanks for all you do here.”

She blushes, adjusts her name badge, and heads to the nurses' station.

"Erick, I think you should question him, and I'll see if I can use my powers to tell whether or not he's giving us the straight story."

"You're handing me the reins? That's not like you. Is there something you're not telling me?"

"First off, I didn't even know his last name. Secondly, I didn't sleep very well. Or more like *at all*. I'm running on a giant mug of espresso and a flicker of hope. I can barely think straight. It's going to take all my focus just to tap into my—"

"Quelle joie! The angel from the accident. Come in! Come in!" Philippe motions to Mitzy and grins broadly. I grab a chair for her, and, as she sits down, I whisper softly, "Kind of seems like you're his favorite, Moon."

Her shoulders droop, but she leans forward and prepares to take the reins she so recently abandoned.

"Mr. Mou— Philippe, it seems like you remember me. Mitzy Moon. We met at the gala."

His head bobs, and he continues to smile at my wife. "Yes, yes. You save my life."

She shakes her head and waves away his comment. "No. No. I was only helping until the paramedics arrived. They were the real heroes."

Philippe sets his jaw and shakes his head in

protest. "Yes, they give me something for the pain, but I remember. I remember everything they say. This bone cuts important blood vessel. The man with the short hair says I should have 'bled out' before they arrive. Whatever you do — this help — this save my life."

Mitzy leans away and swallows hard.

Stepping closer to the recovering man, I make a pass at drawing his friendly fire. "Mr. Moueix—"

"Please, call me Philippe."

"Philippe, we don't think what happened yesterday was an accident. Do you mind if we ask you some questions?"

"Of course. You are correct. It is no accident."

"How do you know? Did you see someone?"

His nod is fervent and fearful. "It is the ghost of Cromwell Pearson's father."

Normally, I would dismiss such nonsense, but with my ghost-hunter wife at my side, it's hard to ignore his comment. "What makes you say that?"

Mitzy leans forward, now barely hiding her concern.

"My sister's husband is an idiot. He comes to France claiming a desire for knowledge of old-world winemaking. Cromwell wants no such thing. He wants to steal and to poach and to buy legitimacy for a winery that makes *pisse de chat*."

"Those are harsh words, Philippe." Dragging

my thumb along my jaw, I struggle to understand. "Why would you say that? I thought he fell in love with your sister when he was in France?"

"Love? This word. He offers my father money, and, in exchange, my father sells my sister."

Mitzy reaches toward Philippe but pulls her hand back at the last minute. "Sold your sister? Human trafficking?"

Philippe flails his arms in the air and winces. "I must remain calm. When I get the excitement — blood pressure — call for the nurse."

Stepping into the hallway, I wave to Tammy, and she hurries toward us.

"It will be another forty-five minutes before we can give you any more morphine, Mr. Moueix. Try to breathe deeply, and I'll talk to the doctor to see if there's anything else we can do for you."

He exhales loudly and makes a mock spitting sound over his shoulder.

Tammy rolls her eyes at me as she leaves, and Mitzy resumes questioning. "Answer my question, Philippe. Did Cromwell Pearson buy your sister?"

"It may as well be this. My father simply calls it a dowry at the time. But I know better. I can sniff the stench of this man a mile away." He scoffs and makes a face like he's smelled burned hair. "I am not about to let my sister follow him to America alone."

"So you became his winemaker to protect your sister?"

Philippe nods at Mitzy and shrugs. The lines in his face are creased with regret.

"Tell us about the ghost, Philippe." Mitzy smiles encouragingly.

Who could resist that smile? I'll never forget the first snarky grin she tossed my way . . .

"Cromwell's father is not the big-hearted man of the stories told with false emotion." He sighs and wrings his hands. "When Carson Pearson is alive, he is cruel, spiteful. He never wants his vineyard to produce anything but the world's finest port."

Taking a step closer, I lift both hands. "Shame we never got to taste that port. The Pinot and the dry Riesling were great."

Philippe waves away my compliment. "When Cromwell adds red and white and sparkling wine — this is when the incidents begin."

Mitzy glances toward me, her smoky eyes alive with interest. I nod for her to take point.

"What kind of incidents?" she asks.

"Things will be rearranged. Things will go missing. Petite accidents with equipment. No one suffers injury, but the accidents only happens with the wines, never the port."

"Well, last night's accident *did* happen to the port. So that kinda blows a hole in your ghost theory, Philippe." Mitzy crosses her arms and leans back.

The hard-working French winemaker leans against his pillow and closes his eyes with an air of defeat. "True. *C'est vrai.* But it does not explain what I see."

"All right, you better start from the beginning, Philippe. What did you whisper to Cromwell at the gala? Why did you and Cromwell go into the fermentation room?"

Mitzy rubs her fingertips together eagerly. It's a struggle for her to stop at two questions. I've seen plenty of times where she'll fire three to five out in a row. Philippe should count himself fortunate.

"*Oui! La température.* I go to the fermentation room to retrieve the barrel Cromwell demands. When I open the door, a wall of heat slaps me. *J'ai paniqué.*" He looks from me to Mitzy and shakes his head. "I panic. The fermentation room is always to be at 21° C." Again, he translates. "This is 70° F. But last night it is too warm. I check the thermostat with haste. The thermostat shows 21° C, but I can feel too much heat on my skin."

Mitzy fidgets. "Why didn't you turn it down?"

Philippe acknowledges her question. "I cannot. My keys, they do not work in that lock. Cromwell is perhaps overly cautious of who he trusts. And he has the only key to open this control box."

"So when you ran into the gala, it was to tell him about the problem with the temperature and that you needed his help to reset the thermostat, right?"

He grins like a proud parent. "You are wise and beautiful. Much like my sister. This can be a deadly combination." Philippe chuckles, adjusts his position in the bed with a groan, and continues. "I return with Cromwell, and he sets about opening the box. I hear the forklift start up on the other side of the rack. This is near the large roll-up door, but this door is not open."

My sweet wife's impatience takes over. "Who was driving the forklift? Could you see? Was it an employee or someone from the party?"

Philippe holds his hands up in surrender. "Please, *Mademoiselle*, I can answer but one at a time."

Mitzy exhales and motions for him to continue.

"The motor is loud. I never hear this forklift make such noise or move with this speed. I see no driver. Has to be the ghost."

Without skipping a beat, Mitzy continues, "What did the ghost do next?"

"He smashes the forklift into the back of this pallet rack and knocks the tun at the top loose! I shout—" His face contorts, and he rubs both hands over his eyes.

"You barely got out of the way in time. You're lucky to be alive, Philippe."

"It happens so fast. I cannot save him."

Mitzy's hand touches his arm and squeezes. "It wasn't your fault. Whatever happened with that forklift, whoever did that, they're to blame. You focus your energy on getting better. Aurélie will need your support more now than ever."

"*Oui*. *Oui*. This is true."

She slides out of her chair, glances toward me, and shrugs.

Stepping beside the recovering man, I shake his hand. "Thank you for your time today, Mr. Moueix. I mean, Philippe. We're looking forward to seeing you out of that bed. I hope you'll be back on your feet soon." With that I lead Mitzy from the room.

As I open the passenger door of the Nova, she pauses and turns toward me. "I didn't see a ghost out there. And that wasn't the only thing that bothered me about his statement."

"Same here. The injury to his leg would indicate he had turned to save himself. If he had truly reached back in some attempt to pull Cromwell out of harm's way, I think his injuries would've been worse, or at least involved one of his arms."

Her eyes glaze over and suddenly snap into focus. "Hey, I meant to ask if you saw where Nettie came from. She was ahead of us — or maybe she was coming from the fermentation room."

Pausing, I struggle to remember the sequence of events. "I don't have the advantage of that playback thing you do, but I think she was just ahead of us."

Mitzy kicks out one hip and shrugs. "If you say so, Harper."

"I do. Anyway, let's grab an early lunch and head out to the winery. Nettie will be expecting us."

My lovely wife pushes up on her tiptoes, slides her arms around my neck, and smirks. "Oh, gosh, we wouldn't want to keep your prom date waiting."

"Laugh all you want, Moon. I'm sure there are one or two stories from your misspent youth you'd rather I not get my hands on."

Her eyes suddenly go wide as saucers, and she slides into the car like a docile puppy. "No need to threaten me, Harper."

Chuckling, I shut her door with practiced force and drive to Myrtle's Diner.

CHAPTER 13

When Odell slides that burger and fries in front of me, everything seems right with the world. "Thanks, Gramps. You really know how to make a girl feel like she's living her best life."

His laughter is rough and comforting, like a well-used recliner with one rogue spring. "I'll let you two enjoy your food. Say hi to Aurélie for me."

My hand stops en route to my mouth, and I struggle to swallow what's already there. "Is there something you need to tell me? Something I should avoid telling Grams?"

He shakes his head. "Not at all. Aurélie comes in every once in a while for a slice of my award-winning pin cherry pie. Shares a little winery gossip and heads out the door. Nothing untoward. Nothing for you or Myrtle Isadora to worry about."

He raps his knuckles twice on the silver-flecked table and returns to the grill.

Glancing across the table at the tall drink of water that is my lunch date, I wag a french fry for emphasis. "I don't know what to think about those Pearsons. I definitely picked up on some negative energy between Aurélie and Cromwell. If Philippe is to be believed, it sounds like Cromwell bought and paid for her when he was in France — rather than wooing her with a grand romantic gesture."

Erick savors a bite of his meatloaf and drags his fork through his mashed potatoes, creating a series of gravy locks and dams. "Yeah, we handled a couple of disturbance calls out there when I was sheriff. Nothing serious. Just some broken bottles of wine and smashed stemware. No one ever pressed any charges. If I could go back and listen to the dispatch recordings, I'm willing to bet we'd discover Philippe made the complaints. He seems pretty protective of his sister."

Erick and I exchange a look that exclusively exists between only children. A wistful regret for siblings that never were. Sure, I have a stepbrother now, but we didn't grow up together. We met through a series of tragedies that left him an orphan. He's a great kid, and I always enjoy hanging out with him, but it's not like sharing your childhood with someone. I guess . . . How would I know?

Long fingers wave gently in front of my face. "Hey, you in there?"

"Yeah. Just thinking about what it would've been like to have a sister or brother."

Erick takes a bite of mashed potatoes and nods.

"Although, after meeting the three Pearson siblings, maybe I dodged a bullet."

He chuckles. "Ready to hit the road?"

Glancing at my plate, I point to the three remaining fries. "Are you insinuating that I would leave these golden beauties behind?"

"Not in a million years. But I figured they'd be long gone by the time I got back from paying the bill."

"Touché."

As we cruise down the winding drive approaching the vineyard, all the gala's magic has seeped away.

The dark sky overhead hosts a gathering of ominous clouds that threaten to spill a legendary winter storm.

All evidence of the festivities has been carted away. No torches, no ice sculptures, and definitely no footmen.

Erick leads the way to the front door and heaves open the massive portal.

The inside is much the same as the outside. Sans holiday decoration.

A nondescript woman wearing little more than a scowl and a goth get-up, straight out of an online ad, refuses to look in our direction.

My first urge is to school her with a quick Myrtle Isadora manners lesson, but all too quickly, I remember my years slogging it out at a minimum-wage job.

Taking an entirely different approach, I stuff a crisp twenty into her tip jar and push aside her fears. "We're not here for a tasting. I'm supposed to meet Antoinette. Any idea where she might be?"

The kohl-rimmed eyes dart toward the greenback, and, despite her commitment to her look, the corners of her mouth twitch into an almost-smile. "She's in the barrel room."

Shrugging helplessly, I venture an additional question for my money. "Would that be another name for the great hall?"

This time, her shy green eyes make contact. "Yeah, we also call it the barrel room, but you're right. I can show you."

I inhale sharply and wave away her offer with a grin. "We got it. Save your energy. Lord knows you'll need it once word of last night's kerfuffle gets out."

Her eyes widen, and for a moment the innocence of her true age leaks through her brooding makeup. "That was hella cray, right?"

"Totes." Language is a fluid beast.

Turning back to my amused husband, I grab his elbow and lead him toward the great hall.

Nettie spies us the second we pass through the archway. "Thank you for coming. Things have been insane. The medical examiner was here for over two hours last night. We thought she'd never leave. Deputy Johnson said there were at least three unauthorized attempts to access the crime scene after she left, and this morning, Paulsen threatened to shut down the entire winery!"

While Erick sorts through which order he'd like to pursue, I dive in. "Paulsen doesn't have the authority to do that. She can lock down the crime scene, but give her some pushback on closing down your business. I'm sure there'd be a heck of a lot of paperwork involved, and I know she's not a fan."

Nettie breathes a sigh of relief and nods gratefully. "Emmanuel talked to Johnson this morning, but the deputy didn't get a look at any of the intruders."

Erick jumps in. "Seriously? Normally, he's a little more observant. Did he fall asleep?"

She shakes her head. "No. Nothing like that. He heard footsteps. Later, he saw a light moving around, and finally, he heard strange noises in the fermentation room. He pursued every disturbance, but, like I said, he never found anyone."

My first thought is there may be more to that ghost theory of Philippe's than I originally thought, but I don't mention that.

Erick surveys the room and steps closer to Nettie. "Philippe didn't seem to be too fond of your father. Is there any chance he had something to do with Cromwell's death?"

Nettie pauses, but quickly shakes her head. "No. Uncle P was protective of my mom, but he put up with whatever my dad dished out. He's had many opportunities to retaliate and never taken any of them."

He exhales loudly. "Okay. If you say so. Philippe claimed there was a problem with the thermostat and said there was a forklift moving without a driver."

"It was hot in there." She chuckles bitterly and rubs a hand on her thigh. "Leon and I moved portable HVAC units into the fermentation room last night after the sheriff told us we weren't allowed to touch anything. The temperature has to be maintained, and we weren't allowed to switch off the main system."

My husband nods. "Understood."

Nettie shrugs her strong shoulders. "We couldn't stand by and watch all that port sour. There's definitely something wrong with the thermostat. Philippe wasn't making that up. The forklift moving without a driver . . . That I'm not so sure about."

Erick waits patiently for more, but I can't hold my tongue. I know, shocker. "Why? Is there a ghost?"

She smiles at me like I'm a toddler. "He really got to you, eh? Uncle P has always had a firm belief that my grandfather's ghost was up to no good around here. The only thing I know about the forklift is that it was parked in the machinery outbuilding when I did my check at 4:00 p.m. yesterday. How it got from there to the fermentation room is a puzzle, but I'm sure the explanation isn't a ghost. Bless his heart, but ghosts aren't real."

Erick nods his support of her theory. While I force a chuckle I don't feel.

He pulls out his phone, flicks to his notes app, and types in a few reminders. "Is there anyone else who had it in for your dad? Enemies, former employees, anything like that?"

She lolls her head from side to side and then becomes stiff as a board. "JR!" She makes a fist, inhales sharply, and then forces herself to relax.

"And who is this JR?" Erick's fingers hover above his phone.

"Junior Rudd. Everyone calls him JR. He's a rival winemaker — if you could call him that. In fact, I'm pretty sure he stole a shipment of grapes that were coming to us from South America."

"Did you report the theft?"

"It was complicated." Nettie grinds her teeth and looks at the floor. "But trust me, JR from Loony Libations is definitely behind this. That man is as amoral as they come. He gives Birch County wine a bad name. All he churns out are cheap hard ciders and barely fermented grape juice!"

"Tell us how you really feel, Nettie." Erick squeezes her shoulder and looks her straight in the eyes. "We'll look into this guy and see if he has an alibi for last night. Can we take another look at the crime scene?"

Nettie lifts her arms and lets them fall to her sides. "Be my guest. There's nothing left — nothing but the — mess."

Erick squints with confusion and leads the way to the fermentation room.

I hang back, not eager to see any of last night's unpleasantness.

He looks inside. "What the—?"

Nettie gestures toward the scene. "Exactly. Paulsen had a tow truck out here this morning. She took the metal rack, the damaged barrels, a— She even wanted to take the forklift. Leon let her have a piece of his mind and forced her to leave it on site. It's our only one." She chokes back emotion. "Sure, we should have a backup, but we don't." Nettie presses a fist to her forehead and takes a ragged breath.

Placing my hand on her arm, I make an attempt at building rapport. "Hey, no one has suffered the slings and arrows of Paulsen more than me. Erick and I will get things solved as quickly as we can, and then she'll be out of your hair. Luckily, Erick took photos of the rack and some other stuff before Paulsen kicked us out. Once we interview this rival winemaker, we'll be back to look at the forklift. You can hang onto it for that long, right?"

Nettie pounds one fist into the other palm. "I can take Paulsen."

I'd have to agree. Nettie is intimidating and feminine at the same time. As her uncle might say, a deadly combination.

My law-abiding husband leaves nothing to chance. "No roughing the QB, and by QB, I mean sheriff. We've got you covered."

Her strong shoulders droop, and she bows her head.

Erick gets directions to Loony Libations and we head out.

Yeesh! I understand that almost-Canada has perhaps more than its share of loons, but I hardly think these majestic waterfowl would appreciate their name being used as a poor pun.

CHAPTER 14

Nettie did not oversell the absurdity of Loony Libations. The gate to the property is guarded by a gigantic statue, in the style of a caricature loon, with a wineglass in one wing and its other wing popping the cap off a hard cider. The cartoonish expression is reminiscent of Daffy Duck, but with the signature red ring around the bird's eye. However, in this context, the ring seems more a result of its obvious addictions than its loon DNA.

Erick struggles to find parking in the crowded lot. Looks like Loony Libations is a big hit with the "tourons" from down south.

We enter the tasting room and a gangly man with stringy blond hair and skin like ancient leather approaches. "What can the loon fly in for ya?"

Oh brother. I better keep my mouth shut or this will not end well.

Mr. Harper, always the mature professional, fields the query. "Good morning. Are you JR?"

The man laughs so hard you'd think Erick showed him a video of a surprised red panda. "Nah! I'm Rex. There's only one JR. I'll get him for you."

Erick turns to me, but I'm miles ahead of him. "This place is crazy. Looks like they're not hurting for business, though. Can't imagine why Nettie considers them competition. They're clearly catering to a completely different class of patron."

He arches an eyebrow and leans back. "Well, well, well, your foray into high society seems to have gone to your head."

Punching him playfully on the arm, I shake my head and scan the room for anything that might pass as a clue.

Nada. Bupkus.

An aging frat boy with a protruding paunch and a backward hat jogs from the back room. "Hey, Glazebrook says you're looking for me. Or, as we call him on Friday nights, Glazed-brook."

He guffaws at his own amazing japery. Don't worry, it's a word I learned from Silas.

Erick extends a hand. "Hi, JR. I'm Erick—"

"Yeah, I know who you are, Ricky. Don't you recognize me, dude?"

My husband's eyes glaze over, as is the fashion in this establishment, and I jump in with a dollop of psychic crack filler. "Of course he remembers, Junior. He's just messing with you. Ol' Ricky never forgets a face. You were a couple years ahead of him and played football your junior year — then you tore your ACL, Right? Or am I thinking of a different JR?"

His tomfoolery catches in his throat, and he scans me from head to toe. "Did you go to PCH?"

The acronym used to throw me, but now I have it clear in my mind that it stands for Pin Cherry Harbor, not Pacific Coast Highway. "Nah, wasn't lucky enough. But Ricky fills me in on the highlights of the good old days."

Erick is barely holding it together next to me, but JR turns, throws a series of rapid, fake punches to my hubby's stomach, and then slaps him hard on the shoulder.

Ricky takes it like a champ. "Great to see you again, JR. How'd your knee heal up?"

JR jumps from one foot to the other like a court jester. "Better than new, bruh. Better than new. I'm so blessed, man. That injury pushed me into skateboarding. I still hit the half pipe every day."

I'm pretty sure JR hits some kind of pipe every day!

Former Sheriff Harper soldiers on. "Hey, can we speak privately?"

Rather than concern, Junior winks conspiratorially. "Follow me, Ricky."

Junior takes us into a private karaoke room that is currently unoccupied and closes the door behind us. "This baby is soundproofed. So we're all good. You know what I'm sayin'?"

Somehow maintaining his cool, Erick replies, "I know what you're saying."

Crossing my arms, I bite the inside of my cheek to keep from losing it and lean back to enjoy the show.

My husband calmly continues. "Did you hear about the incident over at Pearson's?"

Junior shrugs. "I'm not in the uptight text group, dude. They win another gold medal or something?"

Erick shakes his head. "No. Cromwell Pearson was murdered last night."

"Dude! I'm straight up trippin'! That guy hated me or whatevs, but duuuuude!"

"Yeah, the family is pretty upset about it, JR."

Our host-dude places both hands on his hatted head and blows a raspberry. "I gotta get some air. Follow me to the helipad."

Did he just say helipad?

Erick acts like it's a perfectly normal thing to

say, and we follow JR through a rear exit on the far side of a row of fermentation vats.

Outside, the sky seems even darker, but a crisp path has been shoveled through the snow and leads to what indeed looks like a helicopter landing pad.

JR approaches a shiny new outbuilding next to the helipad, types in a six-digit code, and opens the door.

Without a word to us, he disappears inside and returns with — wait for it — a remote control helicopter.

"This is like my Xanax, dude. You gotta focus, like, everything to fly these beasts. Can't have anything else in my brain. You know what I'm sayin'?"

Erick nods. "Yep, I do know what you're saying."

JR launches the copter into the air and expertly maneuvers it above the helipad.

I glance at my husband, shrug with a smidge of irritation, and step forward. "Hey, Junior, I don't mean for this to come out the wrong way, but Nettie hired us to look into what happened. I gotta ask you where you were last night, bruh."

The helicopter careens dangerously, and JR struggles to get it under control. He fails. The copter crashes into the snowbank.

"Bummer. At least it didn't cement face. Right?"

My nonexistent patience is screaming inside my head, but I keep my voice civil. "Yeah, that's great. About last night. Where were you?"

"Chill a sec, dude."

Looking at Erick, I shrug and circle my finger at my temple as I mouth, "Nutter."

JR sets the remote control on the ground, pulls his hoodie over his head, and struggles mightily to extract his ball cap from the wad of sweatshirt in his left hand.

I can't believe his answer comes in the form of partially disrobing.

Once his precious hat is returned to its reverse position on his head, he spins toward us, and Erick and I both gasp.

Spread across Junior Rudd's entire chest is a fresh-as-fresh-can-be tattoo. The vineyard's loony mascot extends from the top of JR's sternum to somewhere below the waistband of his sagging jeans. The wing covering his left pectoral holds a half-empty glass of wine, while the right wing is using a feather to crack the top off a bottle of cider.

"I got this yesterday, bruh. Pretty sweet, right? You can talk to Nikki over at Ink Stained. This bad boy took almost eight hours. I didn't jet out of there until after ten o'clock at night, dude."

Erick feigns appreciation. "That is an impressive amount of ink, JR. We'll follow up with Nikki, but it sounds like you're in the clear."

Junior retrieves his sweatshirt and attempts to shove it back on over his hat. Trouble ensues. To keep from laughing at this clown of a human, I have to bite my tongue so hard I fear I taste blood.

At last, success.

"Hey, Ricky, you ain't the sheriff anymore. What are you doing out here rakin' me over the coals, bruh?"

"I'm not the sheriff, JR. I'm a private investigator hired by Nettie Pearson. Thanks for your cooperation."

JR adjusts his sweatshirt and, for the third time, reseats his hat. "Oh yeah, that Nettie, she's like a handful, you know what I'm sayin'?" He smirks and lifts his chin.

Creeptastic.

Finally, Erick reaches his limit. "I'm afraid I do not. Have a good afternoon, JR." He turns and I follow, always enjoying the view, but especially pleased with the snark.

CHAPTER 15

We walk silently to the car, but once inside, a fierce fit of the giggles grips us both.

Erick is the first to regain his composure. "That was one heck of a tattoo! I gotta say, he seems awfully committed to his brand."

This comment only serves to keep my chuckles rolling. Eventually, as we drive toward Châteauneuf-du-Nord, I pull myself together.

"Wow. That was an experience and a half, Harper. Every time I meet someone from your high school, I'm more and more impressed with how you turned out."

"You can thank Gracie Harper for that." He smiles, but sadness seeps from him.

"Your mom is the best."

"Thanks. When I was over at the house looking

for my tux and the dress shoes — all the memories came rushing back. The house is so empty." He stops and nods to himself. "I'm not complaining about the awesome life we have together. But, she's my mom." His Adam's apple struggles mightily to swallow the welling emotions.

"We should send her a ticket. I mean, there's still snow on the ground, but she only stayed a week at Christmas. Maybe you can talk her into coming out for our anniversary. What do you think?"

His big blue eyes swallow me. "Are you sure? You're not sick of mother-in-law visits?"

"What? Never. Your mom is easier to handle than Pyewacket. She's welcome anytime. That's why we built the second-floor guest suite at the walk-up. Give her a call when we get home."

He eases the car to the shoulder — or as close as he can without getting swallowed up by the heaping snowbanks filling the ditch.

Before I can protest, his arms are around me, and his lips are on mine. "You're definitely winning the world's best wife award this year, Moon."

The next kiss stops time and reminds me how lucky I am.

General nodding and steadying breaths fill the silence as he pulls onto the road.

Erick takes one hand from the steering wheel and rubs my knee. "How come you don't have any tattoos? Seems like that would fit with your rebel persona."

"Random and rude." I playfully brush his hand from my knee and cross my arms. "The truth is, when I was neck deep in my rebellion, I could barely afford to pay rent, let alone waste money on expensive body art."

"Makes sense. My story is, I never got around to it. Lots of guys got inked in the Army. I could never make up my mind. Never really came across anything that I wanted on my body for the rest of my life."

The setup is too good to be missed. "Until you met me, right? I'm happy to be on your body till the end of time."

His cheeks flush an adorable shade of magenta as he turns into the Pearson's winery.

"Keep it professional, Moon. We're on a case."

"Don't blame me. The HR manager forgot to send me to that sexual harassment class."

Erick tilts his head, chews on my comment, and finally shakes his head with a sly grin.

"I knew you'd get there eventually, Harper."

Nettie is stocking the shelves in the tasting room with various wine-based condiments when we walk in.

The goth girl behind the tasting bar catches my

eye over the heads of her full lineup of customers and nods.

Cool. I did that. I made a friend today.

"Well, did you get enough evidence to convict JR?" Nettie tosses a jar from one hand to the other.

Erick drags his left thumb along his lightly stubbled jaw. "Sorry, Nettie. JR seems to have an airtight alibi. We'll check with this *Nikki* at Ink Stained, but, looks like he was in the chair getting a massive tattoo until late last night. Couldn't have been him."

Nettie slams a jar of Chardonnay mustard on the shelf, and several things teeter precariously.

"Gosh darn it! I thought we had him this time. He's such a terrible pain in the neck!"

"Don't worry, we haven't given up." Erick gestures to the fermentation room. "How 'bout you take us back to that forklift now?"

"Follow me." Nettie picks up the cardboard box she was working from and carries it with her.

Mad respect. If that had been me stocking shelves, I'd have left my half-empty box in the middle of the floor and hoped somebody else would deal with it. I mean, that was me then. The me *now* would most likely have done the same as Nettie. Amazing what a few years, financial security, and an altered perspective can do for a gal.

The forklift hasn't been moved. Despite Nettie's claim that it was their only one, the excuse that served as the chief reason Paulsen couldn't remove it from the scene, it looks like no one's been anywhere near this thing.

Erick carefully examines the vehicle while I twiddle my thumbs. Nettie is standing right next to me, so I don't feel comfortable using my extrasensory abilities, and Harper knows way more about motorized vehicles than me.

"Nettie, what's this?" He points to a black box, smaller than a cell phone, under the dash.

She steps over and leans into the forklift next to my husband to get a closer look.

Despite my knowledge of their platonic past, her nearness to my hubby totally registers on my jealousy meter.

"I've never seen that. Maybe it's something to do with insurance tracking?" Nettie steps back and crosses her arms. "Seriously, I just drove this thing yesterday before the gala. I don't remember seeing that."

Erick climbs into the cab of the forklift, flicks on the flashlight app on his phone, and studies the contraption.

Nettie and I collectively hold our breath.

He curves forward, fiddles with a couple of wires, and sits back. A mix of satisfaction and anger wafts off him.

"What is it, Harper?" I lean forward.

He looks at me, and the muscles in his jaw flex. "I'm no expert, but I'm pretty sure I know a remote control receiver when I see one."

The words "remote control" bring up an instant image of Junior Rudd and his ridiculous toy helicopter. "What are you saying? Someone was driving the forklift by remote control?"

He looks from Nettie to me and nods once. "That's exactly what I'm saying. I gotta call Paulsen. Get the boys to take this in."

Nettie opens her mouth to protest, but Erick raises a hand. "Don't worry, not the whole forklift. Just this device."

She breathes a sigh of relief, and Erick places the call. As soon as he hangs up, I step closer and lower my voice. "This could put Junior back in the frame, right?"

He shrugs. "He'd have to have one hell of a transmitter, Moon. The tattoo parlor is over by the community college. Just a guesstimate, but that's over five miles, the way the crow flies."

Nettie wrings her hands and paces. "So, Uncle Philippe was right. There wasn't anyone driving the forklift. No wonder he thought it was a ghost."

I sigh and nod. "Yeah. The ghost theory totally makes sense now. Even though I thought—" My eyes widen and I look to Erick for a bailout.

He gracefully steps in. "I'm sorry to say we didn't believe him, Nettie. But this evidence means it could've been anyone at the party last night. I need you to think really hard about the people on the guest list. Was there anyone who might've had a grudge?"

Nettie rubs her hands across her face and sighs loudly. "Honestly, his own children probably had more of a beef with my dad than anyone else. There's so much fighting in my family. He and Leon were yelling and screaming at each other almost every day. My dad was determined to keep everything old-school, and Leon insisted on using his knowledge of physics to modernize everything he could get his hands on." She places a hand on her chest. "And I'm not trying to push Leon into the spotlight alone. I fought with my dad, too. I told him if he gave me the winery, I would protect the family name. He would scoff in my direction and tell me how only a male heir could carry on the family name. So rude. Even Emmanuel used to fight with him, but once Manny got his degree in hospitality and started plans for the Châteauneuf-du-Nord hotel, he couldn't care less about Dad and the winery."

Erick shrugs his shoulders, and I sense reluctance curling around his spine. "Nettie, I really am sorry to have to ask this. Did you kill your father?"

Her initial reaction is shock and hurt, but she's a

smart woman, and, as she sifts through the facts we have in front of us, she can see how Erick ended up suspecting her.

"It's a fair question, Harper. I certainly had more reason than Leon. He stood to inherit the winery, no matter what. You could argue that killing my father would've made me a rich woman, and maybe I could've bought Leon out. I don't know." She exhales weakly. "But I can tell you, I didn't do this. I wouldn't do this. No matter how much we fight, family is everything to me."

The words are sincere. I feel her commitment to this place and these people.

Erick nods in understanding and apology. "I had to ask, Pearson. Let us know when they pick up the remote receiver. We'll be in touch."

"Thanks, Ricky."

My heart smiles. Every time I hear it. Every time.

CHAPTER 16

SILENCE IS NOT MY SPECIALTY. As we drive back to Pin Cherry Harbor, I have to hash over what we've learned.

"Do you think it's possible Nettie had something to do with this?"

Erick taps his thumb on the leather-wrapped steering wheel. "I have to keep my personal feelings out of this. The Nettie who played football with me back in the day would never do something like that, but I always say that everyone's a suspect until they're not. This case seems like the perfect opportunity for me to put that philosophy to the test."

"Yeah, sorry, hon. If it counts for anything, I believe she's telling the truth about not killing her dad."

"Thanks." He sniffs sharply. "That does help."

"Do you think you can get one of the deputies to tell you what they find out about that remote control receiver?"

"Should be able to. I drop off the occasional box of doughnuts, and they still invite me out for drinks night at Final Destination."

Twisting in my seat to get a better look at the former lawman, I scrunch up my face. "Do you go? I can't really remember you heading out on your own since we got married."

"I went a couple times, when you had bingo with Twiggy. It's hard, though. I'm mostly okay with putting that all behind me and embracing our PI venture, but when I sit there, shooting the breeze with them and hearing about their day-to-day, I miss it."

"Yeah, I get that. How many more hours of apprenticeship do I need before I can get my official PI license?"

Now it's his turn to scrunch up his face in confusion. "Why do you ask?"

A soft smile creeps across my mouth, and I strum my fingers on the dashboard like a marginally evil villain. "No point getting the cart ahead of the horse, or, in this weather, I should say, the sleigh in front of the horse."

He grips the wheel with both hands and pushes back into the driver's seat. "I know we said no secrets, but as long as it's not directly affecting our relationship, I'll allow it."

Gulp. It's best if I keep this seed of an idea to myself until I figure out if it can sprout. "Copy that. Now, how about you answer my question? How many hours?"

"Let's see . . . We've worked several cases together, but you're missing out on a lot of opportunities by not spending more time in the office. We could count that toward your training — if you were there."

"Not gonna happen, Harper. I'll stick to fieldwork. Give me a rough idea of what I'm looking at."

He tilts his head and gazes into the distance. "You've got at least a thousand hours left. Maybe more. Should we head back to the office and figure it out?"

"A thousand? Yeesh. Let's keep it vague for now so I don't lose hope. I'll come up with something."

Erick opens his mouth, but I want to table this whole conversation.

"My tummy tells me it's after lunch. How would you feel about swinging by Bless Choux for a couple slices of quiche and some hot chocolate?"

"Sounds great. After that, I'll drop you at home. You can update the murder wall while I follow-up on some of this technical mumbo jumbo."

The thrill of delicious pastry in my near future

almost snuffs my natural snoopiness — not quite. "What technical mumbo jumbo?"

"I need to find out anything I can about remote-control transmitters. I'm pretty sure Howie Fairlane, the Great White North's only IT Specialist, will be happy to bend my ear for an hour or two on the topic." He chuckles as he turns from Main Street to Third Avenue.

"Better you than me, Harper." I keep my opinion on the IT specialist to myself. Howie is a treat for the eyes, but an Ambien for the ears.

The owner of the patisserie smiles brightly when we enter.

"Hey, Anne. How's business?" I wave like a silly fangirl.

She gestures to her half-empty display case and the crowded seating area, and smiles. "Couldn't be happier. The locals really keep me in business during the off-season. What can I getcha?"

Erick glances at the menu board to ponder his options, but I know exactly what I want. "I'll take a slice of bacon and onion quiche, cocoa with extra whip, and a chocolate croissant."

Beside me, my husband chuckles unnecessarily. "I'll take the same minus the croissant, Anne."

She taps the final prices into the register and grins. "You betcha. Have a seat anywhere and I'll bring it out."

I pull some cash from the pocket of my skinny jeans, but Erick beats me to the punch. "This is my treat, wife-y."

Oh brother. Without taking the bait, I claim the last bistro table. He joins me, and the moment he sits opposite me, an inexplicable flash of Federico the Fantastic, the murderous magician from our first official case, flashes through my mind. When we learned that the magician's real identity was Alex Crenshaw, and that he was Erick's biological father, my husband slammed an Iron Curtain on all his feels. If this man popped into my head, there's probably a psychic reason. Perhaps I'll see how well I can wield an emotional cutting torch.

"Erick, have you given any thought to visiting Alex Crenshaw at the state penitentiary?"

"No. Why?" He exhales and crosses his arms in that yummy way that makes his biceps bulge. However, I can't enjoy the view with all the negative energy flowing from him.

"No reason. It's totally your business. Like I told you before, I support whatever you choose. No pressure, just a question."

His arms remain crossed, and his gaze narrows. "Promise me you're not planning something."

Pressing a hand to my chest, it takes a moment to find words. "Never. I would never do that to you. I remember how hard it was for me to agree to meet

Jacob. Sure, I'm super happy about how things turned out with my dad, but I would never force anyone into that situation."

He walks his fingers across the table and turns his palm up as a peace offering.

I slide my hand into his, and he squeezes tightly. "Thank you. That means a lot to me."

Before our discussion can turn any softer, Anne arrives with a tray of wonder. "Here you go. You let me know if you need anything else." Her ready smile and bright eyes make us feel like family.

"Thank you, Anne. This looks delicious."

She bows with trademark humility and retreats to her pastries.

I start with my chocolate croissant and receive an all-too-predictable snicker from my husband.

"Mind your own business, Harper. Last time I checked, this was a free country."

He pops a bite of quiche into his mouth and savors it silently.

It doesn't take me long to power through my delicious lunch.

"Are you planning on questioning the rest of the Pearsons?" The whip has melted into the hot chocolate, and the creamy mixture delights.

"We'll have to. I don't have much of a relationship with Leon and Manny, but at least they know me. I have no idea how to approach Aurélie." He's picking at his quiche rather than eating it, which is not like him.

"Let me handle the mom. Philippe seems pretty taken with me. If he puts in a good word for me with Aurélie, that should do it." I raise my mug for a "cheers."

He clinks his mug to mine and smiles. "Yeah, you definitely put a spell on that Frenchman."

We bus our dishes, wave to Anne, and load up.

Next thing I know, Erick is stopping on First Avenue in front of the walk-up. As I hop out of the Nova, there's a corner of an envelope peeking out of the mailbox. "Look! We've got mail! Again."

He laughs, pushes in the clutch, and slaps the shifter into neutral. "I'll wait in case it's something for the office."

Hustling up the steps, I snatch the envelope from the mailbox, flip it over and freeze.

"Mitzy? What is it? Who's it from?"

At that moment, my voice eludes me. I want to answer, but there are no words.

Somewhere in the distance, a car door slams.

My eyes are fixed on the return address on the envelope in my hands.

Clearwater.

That's the only word I need to see. My father did fifteen years in the state penitentiary, and there's not much else in that town. Jacob chose to use his experience to better himself, create the Restorative Justice Foundation, and, in turn, better the lives of ex-cons all over the state. However, this letter can only be from one person. Alex Crenshaw. Convicted murderer, and Erick's biological father.

Fingers are gently snapping in front of my face. "Hey, Moon. Did I lose you?"

Silently, I push the letter toward him as a brisk wind stings my cheeks. This former sheriff of Birch County is all too familiar with Clearwater. He's placed a significant number of felons in that prison.

The look on Erick's face when he clocks the address, shows he assumes what I already know.

Alex Crenshaw finally wants to talk.

CHAPTER 17

Gusts of wind buffet around us, and the temperature seems to drop several degrees as the tension thickens.

"You don't have to go. Whatever decision you make is the right one for you. If you want to go, I support that. I'll even go with you if you want—"

Erick silently raises a hand to stop my verbal diarrhea. He slowly shakes his head and shrugs.

New approach. My voice, barely a whisper. My tone, humbly apologetic. "Sorry. Do you want to talk about it?"

He pulls me close, and the frosty wind swirls around us as we stand on the stoop in awkward silence.

"I know you support me, and I appreciate that. I

do." He sighs heavily, and his lips graze my forehead.

Images of my mother rubbing small circles on my back to comfort me after school-day disasters leap to the forefront, and I do my best to mimic the gesture from the memories of a small child.

Losing her when I was eleven leaves me little to go on. Would I have grown to resent her as a teenager? Would there have been arguments and harsh words? Would she have given up on me, or would our trials and tribulations have ultimately brought us closer together? All the things I'll never know. All the questions any orphan must have.

Erick leans away as he groans. I pull my hand back and shove it into the pocket of my puffy coat. Patience is something I severely lack. If he doesn't say something soon—

"Will you be okay without me until tomorrow, Moon?"

"I can handle Grams, if that's what you mean. I'll update the murder wall and see how Silas is doing on the research project. But I'm happy to tag along if you need company on your road trip." I try to contain my over-eager worry. I pretty much fail.

A weak smile grazes his pouty mouth as he slides an arm around my shoulders and pulls me near. "I need to do this on my own. And I need to do it today. It's a three-hour drive to Clearwater. I'll crash at a cheap motel tonight and head over to the prison first thing in the morning. Will Pyewacket be enough company for you if I don't get back till tomorrow afternoon?"

Hopefully, my attempt at a brave tone will fool him. "Of course. Pyewacket and I got along just fine without you when you were busy protecting all of Birch County. We can easily make it through one night."

He kisses the top of my head and continues to hold me tight. "Thanks. I have no idea what Alex wants to talk about. I'd just as soon get it over with. I'm not looking to ignite some relationship with the guy, but if he wants to clear the air about how he left me and my mom, fine by me."

Pretending to be a normal wife and not one with extrasensory perceptions, I force myself to ignore the storm of abandonment issues swirling beneath my husband's carefully controlled exterior. "Yeah. You and Gracie did more than fine. She raised one of the kindest, most well-respected men in Pin Cherry Harbor. Alex Crenshaw doesn't get to take any credit for that. You are your own man, Erick Harper. I'll be all right until tomorrow. Call me if there's anything I can do. Promise?"

He holds me at arm's length and gazes down at me with the purest love I've ever known. "Always."

Swallowing my emotion, I blink back unexpected tears and offer a hasty hug. "You better pull your car closer to the curb and run upstairs to pack an overnight bag."

Busying myself in the kitchen, I make him a peanut butter, honey, and banana sandwich for the road. His favorite, not mine. No judgment.

"Here's some snacks." I hand him a reusable grocery bag with the sandwich, an apple, and a baggie full of Fruity Puffs. The only thing missing is a juice box. Oh brother, I'm definitely working overtime to shove my fears down as deep as possible.

"Thanks, Moon. I'll call you from the motel."

He kisses me softly, but his distraction is evident.

"Bye!" My false bravado has a hollow ring.

He waves and exits.

As the rev of the Nova's engine fades into the distance, my heart drops into my stomach.

The wind howls across the great lake nestled in the harbor behind my bookshop, and the 6 x 6 windows rattle and creak.

When the first blast of this storm hit the building, I abandoned the lonely walk-up and raced to my old apartment.

Currently, I'm huddled on the four-poster bed with Pyewacket curled around me. "Of course

Erick would be gone when the storm of the century hits. You'll protect me, right Pye?"

"Reow." Can confirm.

Grams flickers in and out of the visual spectrum.

"Storm interfering with your energy, Grams?"

"I don't know, dear. I just feel different. Detached somehow."

"Detached? Like you might be pulled through the veil?"

"I can't be sure, sweetie. I'm going to pop out of sight and conserve my strength. Better call Silas tomorrow and let him know what's going on."

My heart is flooding with worry, while my subconscious appreciates the call for help I made a few days ago.

A thin voice calls from the ether. "I knew it! I saw him in here doing research, and he acted rather strange when I passed him a note."

"No. Thought. Dropping." Tugging the comforter around me, I lean toward Pyewacket and long for sleep. Fierce wind whistles, and everything outside the windows blurs to a silver-white.

The blizzard is upon us.

The gnawing unease in my throat is obliterated by a shattering blast from the snow-pocalypse outside.

The bedside lamp pops to black.

Despite my best efforts, a panicked screech escapes, and Grams hovers beside me. "What's wrong?"

"The power went out. The lights are out. I'm not afraid of the dark . . . Necessarily."

"The candles are in that drawer, under the bookshelf where we keep the family photo albums."

Feeling my way in the darkness, I trip over my hastily discarded slippers and launch forward onto the thankfully plush carpet.

I swear to you, there's a feline snicker from behind me.

"Not all of us are blessed with perfect night vision, son."

At last, I make it to the drawer and give it a firm push inward. It pops out, and I feel around until I find candles and a lighter.

When I turn, the shimmering apparition of my grandmother blocks my path. "You could've used the flashlight on your phone, sweetie. Here, follow me back to the bed."

"You're not wrong. Although I should probably conserve my battery. I don't want to miss a call from Erick."

Grams guides me back to the antique bed with no further disasters, and I place two candles on the nightstand. It takes a few clicks of the rusty old lighter, but eventually, the wick springs to flame and the warm glow chases away the darkness.

"Maybe I should text Erick and let him know that the power is out."

Ghost-ma floats closer. "Why would you do that, dear? That will only worry him and give him an excuse to change his plans."

"You're right. You're totally right. I'll just cuddle up with Pye and—"

The fierce storm lashes at the bookshop, and my imagination spins out of control.

"What if the power doesn't come back on? We could freeze to death. I mean, me and Pye. You'll be fine, obviously."

She gasps. "Mizithra! I'm surprised at you. Do you think it would be easy for me to watch the two of you—? I can't even say it!"

"Of course not. Everything will be fine. There's no point in worrying, right? Worrying can't change anything. That's what Silas always says, isn't it?"

Grams flickers and vanishes.

"Grams? Grams?"

Silence.

"Great! Erick is on a road trip, Ghost-ma is having an otherworldly crisis, and—"

Slapping my cheeks with both hands, I exhale loudly and shake my arms to release all this nonsense.

"You know what, Pyewacket? This is going to be a wonderful adventure. My seventh-grade science teacher used to say, 'The only difference between adventure and adversity is attitude.' And I'm changing my attitude right now. I'm a smart, self-sufficient adult, and I can handle whatever life throws at me."

The blizzard slams an immediate challenge to my assumption into the building and the windows screech dangerously.

Sliding deeper under the thick down comforter, I scoot closer to Pyewacket and clutch my phone like a life preserver. "When — not if — Erick texts me, I'll make a nice, sane reply about how happy I am that he arrived safely. No mention of the blizzard or the power outage. I'm a big girl."

The swirling in my tummy and the tight muscles between my shoulder blades beg to differ, but I'm choosing to ignore them.

The minutes tick away. I doze off, but fierce winds and other unidentifiable sounds drag me back to consciousness — repeatedly.

At last, my need for contact with the outside world exceeds my concerns about running down my battery. I wake my phone up.

3:33 a.m.!

Erick should have arrived in Clearwater hours ago. What if the storm blew him off the ro—

Without finishing the thought, my fingers are flying over the keyboard, sending a panicked text.

Beep.

"Message failed to send!"

What the—!

No bars. No service.

Tossing the phone in anger, I curl around Pyewacket and force him to endure my affection.

His black-tufted ears twitch as I scratch his broad tan head and let my tears soak into my pillow.

"There's no cell service, Mr. Cuddlekins. Erick can't reach me. I mean, that probably means he made it all right and his text to me didn't come through. And he'll wonder why I didn't respond. He knows I would never ignore a text from him, right? What if he thinks I'm upset that he went without me? What if he thinks I don't support—?"

A large paw presses against my lips. Pyewacket has had quite enough of my worrywarting for one night.

I lightly push his paw back to the pillow and acknowledge the warning. "Copy that, Pye. We'll deal with this whole situation in the morning."

"Reow." Can confirm.

CHAPTER 18
ERICK

THE DRIVE to Clearwater is far from scenic. A layer of snow blankets everything in our northern region, and that's really all my brain can handle right now. Thoughts and images of my life with my ma are firing off in my head like rounds down a range.

I have no idea what Alex Crenshaw intends to tell me. His letter was vague and pleading.

Like I told Mitzy, I want to get this over with.

Sure, I may have grown up without an official father, but I never noticed. My mom worked hard to give me everything I needed. Whenever I glanced at the sidelines, Gracie Harper and Odell Johnson were there, cheering me on.

Looking back, it's hard to imagine my life without the positive influence of Odell.

Right before my wedding, I found out he and

Silas helped my mother get a quickie divorce when my father disappeared shortly before my birth. Ma reverted to her maiden name, and I became Erick Harper. She didn't see fit to give me a middle name, and, much like my biological father, I never missed it.

Odell, Mitzy's grandfather, and Nimkii, the owner of Chez Osprey on Fish Hawk Island, took me hunting, fishing, and camping. I learned about honesty, integrity, and kindness from both of them. It's impossible to exaggerate how deeply they influenced my life. Glad to say it was all for the better.

The highway has been recently plowed, plus there's not much traffic. Works for me. The way my mind is swirling, the last thing I need is a road filled with tourists or dangerous patches of ice.

Maybe I should prepare a speech. Should I?

When I search the recesses of my brain, there's nothing I want to say to Alex Crenshaw.

My childhood was perfect the way it was. There were some rough years at the end of my second tour in Afghanistan. Had to deal with a stretch of dark days when I traveled across this country, writing the names of my fallen brothers on the back of the population signs in their home towns.

Not everyone came back. That was a reality I learned to accept. I wasn't going to waste the life I'd been given. First time my ma convinced me to run for sheriff of Pin Cherry Harbor, I absolutely thought I would lose. Wasn't until later we found out a hefty donation from Myrtle Isadora pushed my campaign over the top.

Once the sheriff's uniform became part of my life, I had a purpose. Handling the well-being of the citizens of Birch County was my responsibility, and I took my role seriously. Figured I'd wear the badge until retirement.

Then Mitzy Moon walked into my town.

Laying eyes on her for the first time sticks in my memory like it was yesterday.

Answering a call from Tally about a vagrant, I walked into Myrtle's Diner intending to issue a warning and escort the undesirable out of town. When my gaze landed on that snow-white head of hair, those enticing grey eyes, and curves for days . . .

Honestly, a part of me wanted to drop onto one knee right then, but I had a job to do.

Too bad I was too distracted to do it.

I tripped over my own feet, fell backward, and somehow pulled her down on top of me. Well, I knew my fate was sealed.

She sure took her sweet time figuring out her side of things!

Had I known there would be ghosts and psychic abilities involved in the chase, I might've given up. She was right to hold off on telling me everything. That version of me wouldn't have been able to handle a drink from that fire hose.

Some days it's still hard to believe I live with a ghost. How can that be real?

Anyway, whatever happens tomorrow with Alex Crenshaw, it's not going to change the wonderful life I have. I'm not gonna make any room for him, and I won't shed a tear over it.

The trip takes nearly five hours. I keep stopping at truck stops and trying to talk myself out of going. Some part of me can't let go. I have to know what he wants.

Just outside of town, a dim neon arrow peaks through the leafless branches and announces, "Vacancy." Place looks creepy. Mitzy would likely compare it to the Norman Bates' motel from *Psycho*, and she wouldn't be far from the truth. I'll sleep with one eye open.

Pulling into the Clearwater Motor Inn, I grab my rucksack and head to the office.

The door is locked, but a crooked sign in the window claims they're open.

I ring the bell and wait.

A man who is all angles and flannel appears on the other side of the glass. A cigarette hangs from the corner of his mouth, and a 12-gauge shotgun occupies his hands. He stares expectantly.

"Good evening, sir. I need a room for the night, if you've got one."

"What's your business?" The cigarette flaps as he speaks.

Mentioning any relation to a felon seems like a bad idea. "I'm a private investigator from Birch County. I have to interview a prisoner tomorrow."

"Got a badge?"

"No. But I have a license. Hold on." Moving slowly, I extract my wallet and hold it in his view. Removing the PI license, I press it to the glass.

He leans in to get a closer look.

If I were an escaped convict, this would be the perfect opportunity to smash my fist through the thin pane and grab his gun. The carelessness of suspicious people always amuses me.

The license does the trick, and the owner hands me the key to #3.

This place hasn't seen a remodel since 1970. Yellow walls, dirty shag carpet, sunset orange bedspread — complete with cigarette burns — and an avocado-green rotary phone on the nightstand.

Dropping my gear, I fire off a text. "Arrived safe. Motel is sketchy. Miss you already. Call if you want."

After a quick shower, I flick through the three

stations on the ancient television and check my phone.

When I call Mitzy, her phone goes straight to voicemail. That checks out. Her phone probably died and she doesn't realize.

Time to hit the hay. I'll leave the ringer on in case she calls later.

CHAPTER 19

ERICK

Even the lifeless winter sun thinks the motel curtains are a joke. I'm up, checked out, and headed to the adjacent café before 0800 hours.

No message from Mitzy.

Once again, my call goes directly to voicemail.

I'll deal with that after I deal with Alex Crenshaw. Time to go to the prison.

The Clearwater city limit sign looms into view, and about half a mile beyond that stands the Clearwater State Penitentiary, in all its drab grey and razor-wire glory. It draws my attention like an accident you can't look away from.

Despite the number of felons I've helped house in the facility, I've only been here a handful of times.

Parking my copper-brown baby at the far end of

the parking lot, away from any possible door dings, I grab my identification from my wallet and lock everything else, including my cell phone, in my glove box.

The clerk at the check-in window recognizes me.

"Sheriff! I didn't get a call from your office. And you're in your civvies. Is this official?"

A quick glance at the name patch above her pocket helps me recall our previous conversations. "I'm no longer the sheriff, Dominguez. I tendered my resignation last year, and Deputy Paulsen is— Well, she's officially the sheriff now. She ran unopposed in the last election."

Dominguez leans back in her chair and taps her pen on the edge of the counter. "Resigned? I figured you for a lifer, Harper. Scandal was it?"

For some reason, the question makes me chuckle as I picture the walking scandal that is my wife. "Not exactly. I fell in love with an amateur sleuth. One of us— Not important. I'm a private detective now. And my wife and I work on cases together."

Dominguez smiles wider than any prison employee I've ever met. "Don't let anyone in there hear what a big teddy bear you are, Harper. I'll keep that story between us."

"Thanks." I push my driver's license through

the hole in the bulletproof glass. Dominguez logs me in and slides an official badge back to me.

It's a privilege I don't deserve as a civilian, but I appreciate her nod to my years on the force.

The next guard leads me through a series of secured doors, locking each one behind us as we proceed into the bowels of the penitentiary.

They're taking me to the private boardroom, rather than the public visitation area. Having no idea what Alex Crenshaw has to say makes me appreciate the gesture.

When they open the door to the room, a wave of shock and unexpected emotion washes over me. Lucky for me, I'm an expert at hiding my emotions.

The man sitting in the orange jumpsuit looks nothing like Federico the Fantastic, the magician we arrested for a series of murders in Pin Cherry and Broken Rock.

Previously, he had jet-black hair. He must've stopped dying it in prison. His blondish-grey hair is cut short, and when his blue eyes meet mine, it's hard not to imagine I'm looking through an aging filter — straight into a mirror.

"Good afternoon, Mr. Crenshaw." Pulling out the chair, I take a seat opposite, about a foot back from the table. My posture is all business.

He has manacles around his wrists and ankles, chained to the floor and the sturdy metal table, but his demeanor seems to indicate he's as free as the wind. "Afternoon, Mr. Harper." He swallows hard after he says my name, but maintains his pleasant expression.

"I'm here. What is it that you need to say?" A knot forms in my stomach. All I can do is cross my fingers and hope I'm not going to be sick in this windowless room.

Crenshaw gestures with his chin. "Could you ask the guard to step outside?" His voice is barely a whisper, but there's something about the tone that triggers my former lawman senses.

Turning to the balding prison guard posted in the corner of the room, I once again search for the name stitched on the patch. "Clark, would you mind stepping outside? We'll be fine, and I'll knock on the door when I'm ready to leave, if that's all right."

Clark nods once and, without question, steps into the hallway outside the room.

"All right. We're alone. What is it that you need to say, Crenshaw?"

"I'll spare you the speech about my innocence. I'm sure you've heard it all before. But you need to know that Artemis Ward is dangerous. And she's not done."

The nauseous swirling in my stomach kicks up a notch. "Your former magician's assistant is dangerous? You better start at the beginning, Crenshaw."

Alex Crenshaw spins a tale so bizarre that two years ago I never would've believed it. But now that I have Mitzy, ghosts, and some kind of master alchemist in my life, this man's story has a terrifying ring of truth.

"How did she know you had ties to Pin Cherry?"

Alex inhales sharply and looks at the floor. "She did her homework. That's why she searched for me. Artemis was playing a long con from the very beginning. I'd been making a living in Vegas with my magic act, but it wasn't until she joined the show that the tricks really went to the next level."

"I thought you only referred to them as illusions." It's hard to keep the irritation from my voice.

"That was all her. After the way things went down, I'll never be doing another illusion in my life. Except maybe staying alive in this joint."

There's a twinge of sympathy for this man who helped create me, but I'm not about to let him know. "And how did you get from Las Vegas to Pin Cherry?"

"Like I told you, she pretty much took over managing the act and booking gigs. Before I knew it, we ended up at that casino in Broken Rock. We had top billing until that tailor showed up with his siren-song of a voice. Joey Leduc was only too happy to increase the nightly take by tossing that guy into the prime time slot."

My nod is one of thin belief, but he continues.

"I don't remember everything about those days." He tries to hold up his manacled hands before I can offer a protest. "Honestly, I'm not just saying that. It started with just losing an hour or two, but by the time things got serious, there were whole days I couldn't remember. Sometimes, in the shower, I would have a flash of a lucid moment and feel like I could remember something terrible, but—"

"What are you saying, Crenshaw? Do you want me to believe this Artemis Ward was controlling you somehow? That you aren't responsible for the people you killed?" Cursing under my breath, I grind my teeth together. I'm not sure how much more I can take.

"Believe me or not, but that's exactly what I'm saying. Artemis curated my image. She always told me what jewelry and clothing to wear. The only time I ever felt clear-headed was in the shower. Then I would get dressed, put the jewelry back on, and blank. Things would just go blank. I'm not saying you need to try to get me outta here. I'm—"

"Good. Because I have no intention of getting you out of here. Two people are dead because of you. You're exactly where you belong." Scraping my chair back against the floor, I get to my feet and give a firm cop knock on the door.

Before Clark cranks it open, Crenshaw issues one last warning. "She's dangerous, Ricky. And she's coming for you, or maybe that wife of yours. Someone. I know she's not done. I feel it in my gut, and it makes me sick. Be careful, s—"

"We're done here." Slipping past the guard, I stride down the hallway without a backward glance.

There's not a chance I'll give Crenshaw the opportunity to call me "son."

CHAPTER 20

THE SOFT TICKLE OF WHISKERS on my cheek brings good news. The storm is over.

Easing out of my cozy bed, I tiptoe to the windows and peer across the great lake. A massive blanket of white covers everything as far as the eye can see. Last night's cacophony has been replaced by utter silence.

"Grams? Are you back? I'm going to run outside and make a snowman. I know it sounds stupid, but I never got to do it as a kid. I mean, not like a legit snowman."

No response.

"Come on, Mr. Cuddlekins. I'll feed you on my way out."

Practically skipping to the secret bookcase door,

I smile in anticipation when I press the twisted ivy medallion.

Nothing happens. Not one stinking thing.

Glancing at the bedside lamp, a sick feeling constricts my stomach. "Did we turn the lamp off before we went to bed, Pye?"

Running to the nearest light switch, I flick it hopelessly.

"Power is still out!" Throwing myself face down on the bed, I turn toward Pyewacket and moan, "What are we going to do, buddy? The manual control for the door is downstairs. Last time the power went out, I was on the outside of the apartment."

Rolling off the bed, I pace and force my un-caffeinated brain to function. "You have secret passages . . . but even you can't work that mechanism."

Pyewacket deigns to open his eyes briefly, yawns with complete disregard for my situation, and rolls over.

"Grams!" She does not appear.

Retrieving my cell from the floor, I look at the bars. "Nothing!"

The gravity of my situation sinks in like syrup on a hot pancake. I'm trapped in an apartment with no coffee and no breakfast. I have no cell phone service, so I can't call for help. Not that there would be anyone to call, even if I had service. My father and his wife took a Valentine's trip to the Caribbean.

Twiggy is most certainly snowed in at her place and won't be coming in to work today, and Erick—

I refuse to cry.

"I'm a resourceful gal. We'll figure this out."

Reciting the mantra out loud does little for my confidence.

There's still no sign of Grams, and Pye is working overtime to ignore me.

This feels like a dark and dangerous version of *Alice in Wonderland*. Falling helplessly down a rabbit hole, and there's nothing I can do to save myself.

My fiendish caracal jerks his head up from the bed, and a moment later I imagine a faint noise coming from the bookshop.

"What is it, boy?" As soon as the words are out of my mouth, I'm laughing. "I didn't mean to make it seem like you were Lassie. You probably don't even know who Lassie is. Never mind. Did you hear something?"

Pyewacket leaps off the bed and runs toward the secret door.

I join him and press my ear to the wall. Was that knocking? "We're trapped in here. The power is out. Do you know where the manual—?"

Suddenly my throat feels tight. Maybe I should find out who or what is out there before I tell them how to get in.

An unmistakable harrumph floats through the wall.

"Silas! Oh my gosh! I'm so happy! Do you know how to open the door?"

My question is met with the soft grinding of gears and the slow glide of the door opening.

I've never been happier to see anyone in my life. Lunging forward, I throw my arms around his neck. "Thank you. I figured you knew about the manual levers— But— Wait . . . Did you use alchemy to open that door?"

My mentor's intelligent blue eyes twinkle with mischief. "One must stay sharp, Mizithra."

"How did you get here? Everything's under miles of snow."

"A slight exaggeration, I fear. We received one hundred and twenty-one centimeters of snow last evening, which is equivalent to approximately four feet. A far cry from a mile. Most assuredly, Artie will have her work cut out for her, plowing out the town. However, anyone who's lived in these parts as long as I, has a generator and a well-tuned snow-machine."

"Right. Snowmobiles! I didn't even think of that. Did you have to dig your way out?"

He tilts his head and smiles. "I shall let you answer that question in your own time."

Wow. I'm really batting a negative one thousand today. Of course, he didn't have to dig his way out! He's an alchemist. The man simply transmuted snow into water or air or something. "Well, whatever you did, I'm extremely happy to see you. Things with Grams have gotten worse. She vanished last night, and I haven't seen her since. I called out to her this morning . . . Nothing."

Silas glides a hand across his bald pate and nods. "I must engage in a tad more research today. This blizzard allows me the perfect opportunity to focus on the task at hand. Do you have sustenance in the walk-up?"

"Yeah. I mean, there's food in there, but I'd have to cook it."

Silas guffaws until his round cheeks are ruddy and his jowls jiggle like a bowl full of jelly. "Follow me, Mizithra. I can hardly call myself a mentor if I'm incapable of training you in the simple preparation of a meal."

My psychic senses have been frazzled ever since Erick drove away. Silas is doing his best to distract me with eggs, flour, sugar, milk . . . We're making bannock in the fireplace. Whatever that is.

When my phone rings, I nearly pop out of my skin. I answer the call on speaker, as is my custom because of my total lack of privacy, and lean into my concerned wife voice. "The power went out –

Well, it's still out. Then I had no cell service, and I—"

"Mitzy, it's important." Erick's voice is thick with emotion.

"Right. Sorry. We're all good here. Silas— Hey, how'd it go?" Geez! If this is my mouth without caffeine, maybe I should switch to decaf.

There's a lengthy pause on the other end of the line, a heavy sigh, and Erick clears his throat. "It wasn't what we thought. It was worse."

My mentor's expression turns dark, and for the millionth time, I suspect he possesses some type of psychic premonition ability.

"I have to warn you, you're on speaker with Silas and Pyewacket." I leave out the bit about Grams missing in action. Let him assume what he will. "You can tell us anything. We're all here for you."

"Thanks. It's actually because of your grandmother and, you know, your whole *deal* that I even believe anything Crenshaw said."

"Is he trying to control you? You know, magically?"

"Not at all. He claims Artemis Ward was the one with all the power. He doesn't know how she was controlling him, but he's sure that she was."

"So, he was trying to convince you he was innocent of the murders? Did he want you to try to get him out of prison?" My indignation quickly supplants my empathy.

"Not at all. He wanted to warn me."

Silas smooths his bushy grey mustache with a thumb and forefinger, shakes his head, and gestures for me to move the discussion forward.

"RE-OW!" Game on!

"What was he trying to warn you about? In case you didn't hear, everyone on this end is getting a little overexcited."

He chuckles stiffly and continues. "He said she's not done."

Silas paces softly behind me, as Erick goes on to explain how Alex claimed he was being controlled by Artemis Ward and the losses of time Crenshaw can't account for.

"I hate to say it, Erick, but that sounds a lot like a no-good dark sorcerer we've dealt with before."

Erick and I hiss the name out in unison. "Rory Bombay."

I quickly add, "If I didn't absolutely know he was dead, I'd think he was behind this somehow. But Silas seems sure this Artemis Ward chick was after him."

"That makes sense." Erick exhales. "Crenshaw wasn't sure who she was after. He said he felt in his gut that she wasn't done."

"Silas is still here doing research about— I

mean, working on one of his projects. We're all over this. Drive safe."

"Mitzy?"

"Yeah, I'm still here."

"I love you."

Silas exits to the bookstore, and Pyewacket sulks away as though the cheesy romance is too much for him.

"I love you, too."

Erick ends the call, and I hustle after Silas. I have to know if he's got any additional information about Ms. Ward.

Slipping out of the walk-up and into the Rare Books Loft, I take a chair near my mentor and struggle to wait for his take on the details of Erick's visit with his biological father.

"This turn is most interesting. The loss of time is of great concern. It could be that Mr. Crenshaw is simply fabricating a story that relieves him of his mental burden of guilt. However, it is rather interesting that he held his tongue until he was sentenced."

"Right? If he was gonna con people with this whole 'I wasn't in my right mind' nonsense, you'd think his attorney would've thrown that into the mix during the trial."

"Indeed. It may be fortuitous to ferret out the source of this control he mentioned. When Erick returns, I recommend you ask him to offer you additional details of the specifics of the conversation. Perhaps something will trigger a psychic message, which will reveal the means of her malevolence."

"What will you do? What if she's discovered you're the last member of the secret society?"

"I'm not the final member, Mizithra. I am, however, likely to be her primary target at this time. I've uncovered additional details regarding her origin and interesting facts pertaining to her training. I must put my current project on hold to complete what I've begun where Artemis Ward is concerned."

My heart feels like a lump of lead in my chest. This is like my personal *Sophie's Choice.* "You can't. Grams has been missing for almost twelve hours. Your safety is important to me, but saving Grams has to be our primary concern right now. If there's anything I can—"

"I shall continue my research at home. In fact, I fear I must vacate the premises immediately and distance myself from you and the Bell, Book & Candle."

"What? Why?"

"Ms. Ward is seeking to consume those with special abilities. It won't be long before she draws a line directly from me to you. I shall do everything in my power to prevent such an occurrence."

Throwing my arms around him, I inhale the musty scent of pipe tobacco and denture cream as I blink back tears. “You must have some mag— alchemical way to communicate with me, or send me messages. I can’t just NOT hear from you. I have to know you’re all right.” I point at his jacket. “You have something hidden in one of your pockets, right?”

He reaches into his tweed coat and extracts a small pendant from one of his mysterious pockets. The stone is the clearest quartz I’ve ever seen.

Silas cups it in his gnarled hands and closes his eyes. Whatever alchemical working he imparts is silent and secret. When he completes the incantation, he places the pendant in my hand. “Wear this, and it will connect directly with your claircognizance. You will know that I am safe.”

“Thank you. Thank you.” I kiss his ruddy cheek. “Now get out of here, I guess. And be careful, Silas. Artemis Ward is frightfully dangerous.”

“She is. Perhaps more dangerous than—”

“Don’t say his name. Erick and I already had that unpleasant task earlier. I can’t hear that name twice in one day.” Any mention of the wicked man who ruined so many lives with his insatiable thirst for power literally sickens me.

“I shall respect your wishes. If I discover a cure

for Myrtle Isadora, I will construct a means to transmit my findings."

"When, not if, Silas." I squeeze his arm and blink back tears.

With that, my mentor carefully closes the tome he was studying and replaces it on the shelf next to my treasured copy of *Saducismus Triumphatus*. He nods wordlessly and slowly makes his way down the wrought-iron circular staircase.

CHAPTER 21

Sitting around the apartment all day waiting for Erick to make his way safely back to Pin Cherry Harbor seems bleak. What I need is a little risk, with a side of "not a good idea."

Silas mentioned Artie and the snowplow, and that got the eager wheels in my brain whirring. Grabbing my phone, I fire off a text to the amazing woman who manages the plows that restore our city to order after snowstorms such as this.

"Artie, it's Mitzy Moon! I'm sure you're literally up to your ears in snow . . . After you finish clearing out the hospital and the fire department, could you squeeze in a quick pass down the alley between my bookshop and my dad's place? I need to get the snowmachine out of his garage and head out to Nettie Pearson's."

Faster than you can slide off the road in a blizzard, Artie responds. "You know I owe you more than one favor! I've got plows from down south helping me out, so I'll do you one better than a pass down the alley. I'll be at your place in about thirty and take you straight to the winery. I drew the rural cleanup straw this morning, so I'll have plenty to do out that way. Happy to bring you back to town when we both finish."

An incredibly long text for a Gen X-er! Or maybe she's a boomer? Who knows? All I know is that I have an adventure that begins in thirty minutes.

"Grams? Grams, can you hear me? I know you might not have the energy to pop into the visual spectrum, but can you say something?"

Silence.

As far as I'm concerned, Silas can't finish his research soon enough! We've got to figure out what's happening to Ghost-ma and get her back.

It may sound strange to want to keep a ghost from dying, but I've only known Myrtle Isadora as an apparition. Our entire relationship has grown deeper because of the connection I formed with her spirit. Losing that — Well, it would seem like she's actually dead.

Hustling into the walk-up, I discover the trash strewn about the kitchen.

"Pye! Seriously?" The tan demon spawn is nowhere to be found.

It only takes a minute to tidy up. Whatever that caracal is trying to tell me — I wish he'd use his words!

If I'm going to be ready when Artie arrives, I need to begin the layering process. Silk long underwear, snow pants, wool socks, the whole nine yards! Grams would be thrilled.

Thinking of her love of fashion only makes it harder to keep the tears at bay.

I place the final piece of my outerwear right by the front door, so I'm ready to go when Artie pulls up. Then I set about mixing up a large batch of cocoa. Which, for a non-cook like me, involves boiling enough water to accommodate several packets of instant hot chocolate.

Thank goodness the power came back on.

Pouring the mixture into an oversized thermos, I add a few miniature marshmallows and pace expectantly by the front door.

Soon, the unmistakable thrum of a diesel engine nears, and megawatt lights sweep across the windows as Artie's snowplow turns from Main Street to First Avenue.

I finish bundling, shove my feet into cozy snow boots, and head out the door.

Probably should've left a note, but who's going

to read it? Grams is nowhere to be found, and Erick might not even make it home today. I'll be back before I'm missed.

It's not easy to hoist all that is Mitzy Moon waaaay up and into the enormous snow plow vehicle.

"Morning, Mitzy. I hope you've got some something caffeinated in that thermos."

"I made hot chocolate. I can run back in and brew some coffee if you'd rather have that."

Artie waves away my suggestion. "Pshaw. Hot chocolate will do the trick." She retrieves her travel mug from its holder, pops the lid, and holds it toward me. "Fill 'er up. If we don't do it now, there's no chance of getting a drop in this cup once we're on the move."

When I catch sight of the graphic on the side of her mug — "When hell freezes over, I'll be there to plow us out." — my eyes glisten with mirth. "I might need to get that on a T-shirt."

We share a laugh as I fill her cup, and the thermal flask's large outer cap/cup for myself.

Once we're all situated, Artie shifts into first and we're off.

The gigantic curved plow on the front of our enormous vehicle knifes through the snow as though the wall of frosty flakes were warm butter.

A rooster tail of spray blasts off to the right side,

burying sidewalks and, eventually, the ditch once we're out of Pin Cherry proper.

"Do you know the turnoff for the winery, Artie?"

She arches one eyebrow and shakes her head. "There ain't no road in this town that I don't know! I've been all over this county helping out other snow pushers most of my life, dontcha know. Betcha I know ninety-five percent of the roads from border to border. I'll get you there safely."

"I never doubted that." Lifting my *cap* of cocoa, I offer cheers to her abilities and sit back to enjoy the ride.

We stop once to throw a tow strap around the bumper of a stranded motorist's vehicle and pull them back onto the road behind us. Artie is more than twice my age, yet when she returns to the cab of the snowplow after giving the drivers some hot cocoa and reassurance, she's not even breathing hard. What a trooper.

"There's our turnoff." She slows the plow and eases onto a private road.

"I didn't think the city maintained these private roads."

She lolls her head back and forth. "It's a grey area. If we get a storm that goes on for days, sometimes we're too busy with the essential service responses to get out here. A lot of these folks have a tractor or some other large vehicle with a plow attachment for emergencies. Some of the wealthier rural residents pay a fee to the county or the city to be included in a secondary tier of properties serviced by our plows. The storm hit hard last night, but there's not a drop of precipitation on the horizon. We've got time to take care of everybody."

"That's awful nice of you. Does the city pay for the extra gas?" My snoopy brain never tires of questions.

Artie applies a thick layer of balm on her thin lips and shakes her head. "We have a little endowment. Families of plow drivers will often make donations or even leave us a little cash in their will. It's enough to help us do what we love and serve the community."

"That's wonderful." Note to self: talk to Silas about making a donation to the snowplow endowment.

"Here you are, Mrs. Moon." She winks, and I can't hide my grin.

"Thank you. I have some things to chat with Nettie about, and I'm sure she can entertain me with a flight or two of tastings if we run out of things to talk about. You go ahead and take care of whatever you need to. No rush on my account."

Artie gives me a hearty thumbs up and plows away as I trudge down the recently shoveled path.

The door to the winery is unlocked, but the tasting room is empty. No employees and no patrons. Makes sense. I'm pretty sure this would be considered an official snow day for school and work.

Making my way to the fermentation room, I stop when I hear raised voices. Unfortunately, they're arguing in French.

I recognize Nettie's voice . . . Hmmm, the other voice is male. Philippe is still in the hospital. She has to be arguing with one of her brothers. In a perfect world, a psychic would be able to understand the intention behind the words. Kind of like an inline translator.

Why the heck not? I can almost see Silas steepling his fingers and bouncing his chin in preparation for a lesson.

Taking a deep breath and finding my inner focus, I work on turning my thoughts toward what the words mean, rather than the literal language.

In a moment, Nettie's flow of French begins to make sense. She's shouting.

"You shouldn't have touched the thermostat, Leon. I have a repairman coming to take a look at it and report to the sheriff."

"Petty Nettie! Always so eager to do the right thing to please precious Papa." Leon's voice is thick with disdain.

Excitement over being able to understand their French temporarily knocks me off my game.

A few deep breaths, renewed focus, and I pick up the conversation.

"It doesn't matter what you think, Nettie. The winery belongs to me now. I'll do what I see fit. And I plan on modernizing everything. I can squeeze millions out of this place if we speed up production."

"At the expense of quality? At the expense of our family name?"

Leon's laughter is sour. "Our family name? Don't kid yourself. Everything the old man did was bought and paid for. Including our mother."

There's a strangled groan, and I move closer with the hope of helping Nettie. However, when I catch sight of what's happening in the fermentation room, Nettie has her hands around Leon's throat.

"Oh, and you would know everything about buying women, wouldn't you! That ridiculous trophy wife of yours, bleeding you dry and demanding more. Why on earth do you keep her around, Leon?"

His eyes are watering, and he's in no position to reply.

Nettie must realize what she's done. She shoves him away and rubs her hand over her face. "Leave Mom out of this. She's suffered enough."

Leon coughs, rubs his throat, and his gaze turns deadly. "You should probably look for another job. I don't need someone so unhinged managing my vineyard. For all I know, you're the one who killed Dad."

Nettie turns to leave the fermentation room, and I become acutely aware of my exposed position.

Time to act like I just arrived. "Nettie? Nettie, are you here? It's Mitzy Moon. Anyone here?" Lame. But it's the best I can do under the circumstances.

She blasts through the heavy swinging doors, rolls her shoulders back, and struggles to slow her breathing.

"What are you doing here? How did you even get here?" Her anger isn't aimed at me, but it's at the boiling point. Of that, I'm sure.

"Oh, the snowplow operator is a good friend. When I told her I needed to see you, she gave me a ride out. I thought today would be the perfect opportunity to poke around and interview the family."

Leon storms out of the fermentation room, clearly about to unload further insult upon his sister. When he catches sight of me, his entire demeanor shifts.

The sleazy, lecherous flirt from the gala slinks toward me. "Mitzy Moon. Your hair is different. Is that you in there? I wasn't aware we were to be honored by your presence today." He looks me up and down, searching for the fetching woman in red.

"It's an ongoing investigation." My tone is curt.

"Can I show you around? Or perhaps interest you in a private tasting?"

"I'd love to chat, Leon. I was just telling Nettie that the snowstorm gave me the perfect opportunity to interview the family. Why don't we head into the tasting room and you can answer a few questions?"

He swallows with difficulty and leans away. "Why would you need to question me? I'm the legal heir."

"You sure about that? Have they already read the will?"

His brow furrows. "Next Monday, but I stood to inherit the winery no matter what happened. Cromwell was quite clear about that. What possible reason could I have to kill my own father?"

"No idea." I shrug. "And I'm not saying you're guilty. Just wanted a quick chat."

He glances at his phone and clears his throat. "Sorry, I'm quite busy. I don't have time for a chat."

As he walks away, I call out, "That Givenchy your wife was wearing at the gala was from the current line. That must've had a hefty price tag. Was your piece of the winery pie large enough to cover her expensive taste, or did you need the whole pie?"

He turns on me like a cornered jungle cat, and

his dark eyes blaze with an unspoken threat. "If you're simply looking to accuse people based on their shopping habits, maybe you should start with my mother. Not a day goes by that a truck doesn't backup with some inane and ostentatious delivery for her. Did you know she had a five-million-dollar life insurance policy on my father? Maybe you should have a little chat with her." Leon stalks out of the winery.

Nettie timidly grips my arm. "I hate him. He threatened to fire me! Leon plans to kick me out of the winery I helped to build. This is exactly why I wanted my father to change his will."

"Did he? Did Cromwell change his will?" My senses are poised for a new lead.

"I have no idea." Nettie wipes the tears from her cheeks and sighs. "You should leave. It's not a good day."

"Nettie, I know you're grieving. And I am sorry for your loss — For losing the winery. I realize you weren't close with your father." I offer a head tilt-nod, like the ones I received after my mom passed away. "The large life insurance policy is suspicious. I should definitely talk to your mom."

Nettie's eyes flare with the fire of vengeance. "You leave my mother out of this. That woman is a saint! The things she put up with—"

Reaching a hand toward her, I intend to pat her

shoulder as I'd seen Erick do so many times. However, she leans away and slaps my hand from the air. "You should go."

"Like I said, I got a ride out here with Artie. I don't have a ride back until she finishes plowing the roads. Mind if I have a seat in the tasting room?"

"Do whatever you like, but stay away from my mom."

Nettie stomps back into the fermentation room, and I saunter toward the empty tasting room.

CHAPTER 22

As a former barista and short-term undercover bartender, I know my way around behind most counters. Grabbing a glass and some of the winery's famous Pinot, I take a table in a dim corner. I wish I could say the fireplace was crackling, but the large room is lacking in ambiance today.

I'm three sips into my first glass when my phone rings. Tapping it on speaker mode is second nature.

"Mitzy? Where are you? Are you hurt?" Erick's tone barely disguises his panic.

Oops. Guess I should've left a note. "I'm fine. I'm at the winery. I didn't think you'd be able to make it home, so I—"

"Geez, Moon. You've got to let me know what's going on. We work in a dangerous business, and you take unnecessary risks by nature, but you gotta think about my old ticker."

"Don't be silly, Harper. You're in great shape, and you know I always land on my feet."

His laughter is quick but tight. "Sure, what worries me is from what height? Sit tight. I'll grab your dad's snowmachine and be there in about twenty minutes."

"Seriously? I can come back with Artie." I despise sitting tight — whatever that actually means.

He sighs long and loud. "So that's how you got out there. Couldn't figure out what had happened when I saw your Jeep was still here. Artie will be plowing for hours. I'm coming to get you and there's nothing you can do to stop me. Shoe's on the other foot now."

"Don't you mean the snow boot is on the other foot?"

He laughs, and I sense the relief in his tone. "Don't get yourself into any trouble. I'll see you soon."

"Trouble? How much trouble could I possibly get into?"

The call ends.

As I finish glass number one and pour glass number two, a long, lean woman creeps through the vine-adorned archway from the fermentation room. She glances over her shoulder multiple times and sneaks behind the bar. The weak winter sun filtering through the stained glass windows illuminates the fatigued face of the once beautiful Aurélie Pearson.

"Mrs. Pearson, just wanted to let you know I'm here. Don't mean to startle you."

She carefully controls her features, but the distinct scent of fear hangs in the air. "Who is there? This is not open today. What are you doing?"

"Your children left me to my own devices, Aurélie. I'm currently waiting for my ride, and I helped myself to a bottle of Pinot. I'm happy to pay for it if you know how to run the register." Lifting my nearly empty glass, I nod and smile.

She pulls a bottle from under the counter, expertly spins a wineglass in the palm of her hand and snatches the stem with a level of coordination I could never dream of achieving. "It's Mitzy, no?"

"It is."

"May I join you?"

"I'd say be my guest, but it's your winery. I guess you can be your own guest?"

Her laughter is harsh and filled with resentment. "It has never been, nor will it ever be, my winery. My husband only ever desired the panache a French wife would bring him in this godforsaken northern town. Philippe and I will return to France the moment the funeral is over."

"How is Philippe? He suffered quite a serious break. What did the doctor say?" She speaks much more fluent English than her older brother. Perhaps being a trophy wife is not as easy as one might assume.

She gracefully slips into the chair opposite me and pours herself a generous portion of port. "My brother is strong. I believe your word is resilient? He is this. He has survived worse." She takes a shaky gulp of port, unable to steady her hand.

"Aurélie, what can you tell me about Cromwell? Why was he so against leaving the winery to Nettie? She seems to have a passion for winemaking." Holding my glass up to the light, I gaze through the deep claret liquid, smile, and nod with appreciation. "She really does know how to make an excellent wine."

Aurélie finishes her first glass of port and quickly pours a refill. "She is an amazing girl. Philippe taught her everything he knows. He had such belief, such a trust. They were inseparable."

Her voice is tender when she speaks of her daughter — or maybe the tenderness is for her self-appointed protector. "I hate to ask this, but do you think Philippe could have hurt Cromwell?"

She lifts her glass of port, stares into it for a moment, and downs the liquid in one gulp. "Someone should've done this long ago. That man was poison.

Cromwell poisoned everything he touched. Everyone who ever entered his life. Philippe tried to take care of me. There are limits to what a brother can do."

My special abilities are somewhat fogged with intoxication, but her words seem genuine enough. Plus, Philippe didn't strike me as the murderous type. "What about Napoleon's wife? I'm ashamed to admit I was eavesdropping on a fight Leon and Nettie had earlier. Sounded like your daughter-in-law is a bit of a gold digger?"

Aurélie lets her head fall back as she laughs with true feeling. For the first time since she joined me, I sense her guard lowering. "The rumors about you are true. You see far more than the surface. Perhaps there's a bit of the old crone in your blood, Miss Moon." She sips on her third glass of port.

"It's Mrs. Moon. But I hear what you're saying. I've always been observant. What do you think of my theory?"

"Kylah is capable of one thing and one thing only: handing the credit card to a store clerk. She married into money because she loves money. She thought this would be a larger — how do you say — piggy bank?" I nod at her word choice, and she continues. "And she's held that against Leon ever since she discovered the purse strings could be pulled tight."

A cryptic answer, if ever there was one. "So Philippe is innocent. Kylah is innocent. What about your children? Nettie seems furious with Cromwell."

"Everyone is angry with Cromwell!" She downs glass number three and refills. "Nettie is passionate and has a short fuse, but killing Cromwell would only have hastened her own death."

"I'm sorry? Do you think someone is trying to hurt Nettie?" My antennae try to tingle, but the wine has me buzzing for other reasons.

"No, no. This was — what is the — metaphorically speaking? This is correct, no?"

"Sounds correct. She said Leon was threatening to fire her."

"*Oui. Oui.* This is what I mean. He wants to remove the old ways. You will be pleased to know Philippe is not returning to this hideous abomination."

Wow. Seems like the port is helping her tell me how she really feels! "May I ask you a very personal question?"

There's a glassy glow in her ocean-blue eyes, and she holds my gaze without wavering. "I'm happy to answer any question you might have."

"Thank you. I understand there's a five-million-dollar life insurance policy on Cromwell. You're the beneficiary. I also happen to be privy to the true origin story of your fictional French romance. Simply taking those facts into account . . . You had a reason to want him dead."

Aurélie laughs like a young girl enjoying her first cappuccino and croissant in Paris. "This is the first I'm hearing of any insurance. I hope it is true." She reaches across the table and gently touches my arm. "Mitzy, what you and Erick have is more rare than an 1869 Château Lafite Rothschild. What Cromwell and I had was cheap. An illusion paid for by the patriarchy."

My heart goes out to this woman trapped in a marriage of her father's design. "I'm so sorry, Aurélie. You're a wonderful woman. I wish things had been different for you."

She swirls the port in her glass while a single tear trickles down her cheek. The lines of age have stolen more than her youthful beauty. There's a hopelessness that hangs about her like a dark cloud. "If I had the courage to do what you say, to kill my jailer, why would I have waited so many years?"

Quiet sobs shake her shoulders, and I place my hand on top of hers to offer some comfort. "Sorry . . . for all of it. For having to bring it up. I know you and Philippe will be so much happier in France."

She sniffles and gazes at me with the first spark

of hope her eyes have likely seen in decades. "*Oui*. So much happier there."

"Let's change the subject. Move away from family for a moment. Do you know about JR and Loony Libations?"

She turns and pantomimes spitting over her left shoulder. "Hideous man! Stealing the grapes. Using harmful chemicals on his grapevines. Surely some of that blows onto our precious vines. And that cartoonish mascot!" She sighs dramatically and gazes heavenward.

"Any reason to think he could've had anything to do with Cromwell's death?"

She becomes quite still before tilting her chin upward. "*Oui*. You must speak to him. You must tell the sheriff. This could be! This . . . Oh, my poor Wellie."

That was a heck of a one-eighty. A moment ago, she wished she had the courage to kill Cromwell sooner, and now she feels sorry for the dead man. I can't keep up.

As I open my mouth to continue, the front door blows open, and Detective Too-Hot-To-Handle fills my entire field of vision.

"Of course you're into the wine." He chuckles.

"Hey, no judgment. Aurélie gave me permission."

He dips his head in that way that insinuates

he's doffing a cap. "My condolences, Mrs. Pearson. How are you holding up?"

She lifts her glass, fills it with another glug of port, and takes a gulp.

"Understood, ma'am." Erick shifts his weight. "Sheriff Paulsen stopped Emmanuel at the airport last night before the storm hit. Were you aware he was headed out of state?"

The alcohol flush drains from her cheeks, and, even in the dim light, I can see fear-dilated pupils. "Manny? Why would he leave us before the service?"

Erick shrugs as he walks toward us. "That's what they intend to find out. Anyway, I thought you should know." He takes the coat from the back of my chair and holds it out. "Come on, Moon. We need to get you home."

"10-4." My balance is questionable as I attempt to get to my feet. I'm definitely feeling that third glass of Pinot. Slipping my arms into the coat, I let him zip me up and slide my thick leather choppers on as though I'm a small child. He kisses my nose, takes my hand, and turns once more to Mrs. Pearson.

"We'll be back tomorrow to talk to Manny. They should release him once the roads are clear. If you think of anything, you can call us anytime." He hands her a business card and hustles me out of the winery.

As he loads me onto the snowmobile, I scrunch up my face in confusion. "We have business cards?"

"You are literally the best thing that's ever happened to me, Moon. Hold on tight. I don't plan on taking it easy on you just because you're a newbie."

The snowmachine roars to life, and I grip my arms tightly around his waist. Erick races around the curved drive and out of the winery.

The ride home is a heart-thumping extreme sport. Erick sails down the road, jumps over any available snowbanks, and generally drives like a teenager in a stolen vehicle.

When we finally turn down the alley and park the machine back in my father's garage, he's grinning from coast to coast. "Your dad definitely knows how to tune a sled. Man, that thing runs great!"

"Well, he was eight-time champ of some snow race thing-y." Brushing the snow from my scarf, I chuckle. "That was one wild ride, hubby."

He scoops me from the sled and carries me toward the alleyway door to the bookshop. "And it's not over yet, Moon."

The heat that rockets through my body could melt all the snow in the tri-state area!

CHAPTER 23

"Who's calling at this hour!?" Pressing my head into the pillow with my left hand, I grimace at Erick.

He grabs the phone, covers it with one hand and mouths, "It's How-to Fairlane."

He hurries from our bedroom to the cozy sitting area adjacent to the stairs.

Normally, I'd rollover and go back to sleep, but intrusive thoughts of Ghost-ma instantly lock my brain in "awake mode."

Rolling from the bed with a groan, I splash some cold water on my face, drag a brush through my white haystack of hair, and stumble to the closet.

Today's outfit will include a long-sleeved T-shirt, my favorite skinny jeans, wool socks, and snow boots when we leave the house. Today's tee reads: "I don't rise and shine. I caffeinate and hope for the best." Above a picture of a frazzled kitten.

When I exit the bedroom, Erick wraps up his phone call and launches into an explanation. I rub my eyes, point to my T-shirt, and hold a finger to my lips.

"10-4, Moon. I'll be down in a minute." He heads to the bedroom to change.

"Meet me over in the apartment. I want to update the murder board and hopefully draw Grams out of the ether."

He silently walks toward me and hugs me tight.

His unspoken support means everything to me.

Pushing brew on our too-fancy coffee maker is all I can manage today. Erick joins me, and I pour two mugs for our convoy through the bookshop and across the Rare Books Loft.

Inside the apartment, I cross my fingers and call out. "Grams? We need to update the murder wall. Are you going to fill out the 3 x 5 cards, or should I?"

Nothing.

Erick grabs the stack of cards and the pen. "You say whatever's on your mind, and I'll fill these in."

Sharing the details of my adventure at Châteauneuf-du-Nord, my psychic brain draws some additional connections.

"I got the feeling that even though Aurélie didn't care for Kylah, she identified with her on some level. And despite everything Cromwell put Aurélie through, she was still upset when she thought JR might've been his murderer."

Erick makes a couple of notes as I pace in front of the board.

"Would you like to hear what How-to had to say?"

I'm one cup of coffee into my morning, and I feel like I might actually be ready. "Was it about the case?"

He reclines on the settee and taps the pen on the index cards. "Yeah. Fairlane did me a solid. Paulsen reached out to him to analyze the receiver they confiscated from the forklift. He's the only guy around who knows anything about high-tech electronics. Since I'd been picking his brain about that a couple days ago, he thought it was a weird coincidence and called to update me."

"Sweet. What's the scoop?"

"Fairlane said the receiver is for short-distance transmissions only. He's confident the transmitter couldn't have been more than fifty yards from the receiver at the time the forklift was activated."

Stopping in my tracks, I turn toward Erick. "Hold on. That means every single person at the gala is a suspect again." Flopping onto the king-size bed next to Pyewacket, I absently stroke his tan fur. "Back to square one, Pye."

Erick walks to the murder board and makes a note on JR's card. "I'm crossing JR off the list. He wasn't at the event, and he has a solid alibi. Now that we've determined the transmitter isn't long-distance, it eliminates him. He couldn't have triggered the forklift from the tattoo parlor."

Replaying a psychic memory of the forty people at the gala, my brain goes into overload and I blink rapidly.

"You okay, Moon?"

"Yeah. I keep trying to place everyone at the time of the accident. I can't. I didn't have that much wine, but I guess it was enough to impair my abilities." Scratching between Pyewacket's black-tufted ears, I bemoan our situation. "What are we going to do, son? I've got nothing. And you haven't been very helpful in this case."

His head instantly pops up, and his glowing golden eyes fix me with reproach.

Pye saunters to the murder board, lifts on his hind legs, and returns with a strip of paper in his teeth.

"What's this?"

Extracting the paper from his dangerous fangs, the memory comes flooding back. "Oh yeah, you gave this to me when I was trying on gowns. But this is about you and Grams, and your unbridled shopping addict—"

Everything in the room stands still. Aurélie's words echo in my ears.

Erick waves his hand in front of my face and grins. "Care to share?"

"Remember what I told you about Kylah being a gold digger?"

He shrugs. "Yeah, but you said Aurélie didn't suspect her of being able to do anything other than shop."

"Exactly."

Erick lifts both hands in the air and furrows his brow. "Hey, you can't just say exactly and expect me to be able to read your mind. That's your area, not mine."

"Right. Sorry. That Givenchy gown she wore to the gala easily cost $10,000. If she had a shopping habit like that, Leon might've been more desperate than we assumed. Sure, he stood to inherit the winery no matter what, but Aurélie mentioned the purse strings could be tightened. Cromwell wasn't letting anyone at that money while he was alive. If you combine the motive of wanting to change everything because you're a bitter physicist forced to take over the family business, with an out-of-control shopaholic wife, that could drive a man to take desperate measures."

Erick drags his left thumb along his stubbled jaw. "Solid point, Moon. I've seen people kill for less. Sadly." While I tack the receipt to the murder board. He returns to the settee. "Problem is, we have no evidence. I'll call Deputy Johnson to see if he has any update, but if they found fingerprints on the transmitter, chances are they would have already arrested Leon."

"Solid point, Harper. But what about the pallet rack? I can't imagine someone being able to saw through the steel pallet rack without holding onto the bar or whatever."

He wiggles his fingers in my direction. "Gloves. Anyone as smart as Leon had to think about wearing gloves."

"Maybe. Maybe desperation clouded his judgment. Call Johnson and see what you can find out. We need to get back out to that winery."

My brilliant husband locks eyes with me. "No one's found the transmitter yet. That could be quite incriminating."

Lifting my mug, I shout, "Road trip!"

Then I glance in my cup. "Refill, then road trip."

"Whatever you say, dear." His smile is light, but his gaze smolders with memories of last night.

Struggling to ignore the unspoken message, I press on. "I was thinking we could mix things up and have breakfast at the diner." Erick joins me at the front door, still buttoning his flannel shirt. Yes, I take a peek at the washboard abs being covered in a cozy layer of fabric, and my mind wanders.

"Mix things up? Don't we pretty much always have breakfast at the diner? Unless I make pancakes here." He tilts his head and waits for what I'm sure he assumes will be agreement.

"False. Last time we had breakfast together, it was at Bless Choux."

He pulls me close and brings his lips within a breath of mine. "False. That was an early lunch."

Oh brother! We're never going to make it to breakfast at this rate.

He grabs my coat from the closet and holds it while I slide my arms in. Being the currently sober, independent woman I am, I handle my own zipper and mittens today.

The streets are plowed and, sometime before I got out of bed this morning, my handy husband shoveled and salted our sidewalk.

However, the short walk to Myrtle's Diner becomes a game of snow-bound hopscotch since many of the businesses on Main Street are no longer in *business*. Portions of the sidewalk are shoveled and/or salted and portions are not. Perhaps it's more like being the knight in a game of chess. Move one over to the street, two up and one back to the sidewalk. I don't actually know that much about chess. Now that I think about it, that sounds like too many moves.

The welcoming warmth and scrumptious aromas of Myrtle's Diner embrace us as we push through the door.

Odell gives the standard spatula salute from behind the grill as we slide into our favorite corner booth.

Tally is at the ready with two steaming mugs of go-go juice, and I circle my hands around the plain white porcelain mug. "So, we head back out to the winery, and what? Search for the transmitter?"

Erick takes a long pull on his java and smiles with satisfaction before answering. "Yeah. I guess. Do you think—" he lowers his voice "—your special abilities can help us?"

The first hit of caffeine kicks in and loosens an idea in my brain. "Hey, what if you talk to Nettie, or whoever, and I snoop? Play to our strengths. You know?"

His laughter warms my heart. "Oh, I know. I don't *like* that I know, but I also don't have a better idea, so we'll do that. As long as you stay out of trouble."

I paint my features into the portrait of innocence. "Me? Trouble? Never."

Odell arrives with our breakfast and, after he

slides the plates onto the table, he lingers for a moment. "Hey, can I ask you something, kid?"

Squeaking across the red-vinyl, I pat the spot next to me on the bench seat. "Take a load off, Gramps."

He grins and sits beside me. "I stopped in to check on Myrtle Isadora after the storm. Place seemed empty. Even the cat was MIA."

Bugger. Bugger. Bugger. Suck it up and tell him you've got things under control. "Gramps, I don't want you to worry."

The crow's feet around his eyes deepen. "Well, now I'm even more worried than I was before."

"Silas is working on it. Something's going on with Grams. She's been fading in and out. Getting weaker. I haven't seen her for a couple of days."

The muscles in his jaw flex as he grinds his teeth together. "Boy, I knew this day would . . . Getting her back — getting this afterlife version of her back — I knew it was too good to be true."

"Don't say that. I've got everything riding on this. If there's any possible way we can strengthen her tether or whatever, Silas will find it. He's never let me down before."

Odell slings an arm around my shoulder and hugs me tight as he kisses the top of my head. "I figure between him and whatever you've got going on in that big brain of yours, you'll save the day.

You've never let me down — either of you." He slides out of the booth, raps his knuckles twice on the Formica tabletop, and returns to the kitchen.

Erick's pancakes are nearly gone, so I hastily shake Tabasco onto my breakfast and start shoveling.

Trust me, I always welcome the distraction of vittles.

CHAPTER 24

My thoughtful husband thankfully avoids the topic of Grams on the ride out to the winery. We discuss our strategies for distraction and detecting, and I appreciate his efforts to keep my mind off those otherworldly problems.

"I'll try the mood ring. If it's in the mood, pun intended, I might be able to get some useful information. If we can find that transmitter, that would really help us."

"Maybe. If it turns out to be as clean as the receiver, it might not be of any use at all. Deputy Johnson said they're trying to track down the manufacturer or distributor. See if they can find out who purchased it. The model is pretty common. I'm not holding my breath."

The tasting room is open for business today,

and there are a couple of tourist vehicles with out-of-state plates parked in the slots on either side of the entry.

"I'll look for Nettie. It's probably best if we don't enter together. Otherwise, she might notice when you slip away."

"Copy that."

Erick heads to the tasting room, and I move toward an outbuilding. Entering the huge metal Quonset hut, I plead with the antique mood ring on my left hand and see where it gets me. "I really need your help. We've got to find that transmitter. Could be the difference between solving this case or letting a murderer walk away. I know you want to help me. Please. Wake up and get on the job."

In the past, my ring and I have played a game of psychic hot and cold. Lifting my left hand as I walk around the Quonset hut, I wait for assistance. None comes. Using the other abilities at my disposal, I reach out and see if there are any extrasensory hits.

No such luck.

Heading from that building, I move toward another large metal building with a crazy-sloped roof. The one I just left was curved more like a half-circle or half-oval. This one is practically an A-frame.

The door is locked, and there are voices inside. They're speaking English, and I don't recognize the tones. Maybe this is some sort of vacation rental. Better hot-foot it away from here before someone sees me and reports an intruder.

Moving around to the far end of the tasting room and adjacent fermentation area, I enter a room filled with immense metal equipment. Fortunately, the phrase grape press floats out of the air and gets grabbed by my clairaudience.

Makes sense that the pressing room would be empty this time of year.

Rubbing the smoky cabochon on my mood ring, I once again beg for help. There are all sorts of nooks and crannies in this room. Seems like it could be a perfect hiding place. Plus, it isn't that far from the scene of the crime.

Combing over nearly every inch of the room, I find absolutely nothing. Suddenly, I get the bright idea to check inside the press. Probably a great place to destroy evidence.

I'm not super mechanical, and I know nothing about grape presses, but it's not running and there's no one in here. Not to mention, the handy ladder built right on the end of the cylinder seems like an invitation.

Climbing into the enormous stainless steel tube, through a hatch in the top center, I swing the mood ring hand from left to right and have to admit it holds no secrets.

The roar of an engine and the spinning movement of the cylinder knock me off my feet. I struggle to crawl with the twisting motion like a hamster on a wheel.

I'm not ashamed to say I scream loudly.

"Hey, there's someone in here."

The spinning does not stop.

A sick feeling hits me in the gut. Maybe whoever turned on the machine knew I was in here.

I'm barely keeping up with the rotation, but that's not the bad news.

Some type of thick rubber membrane that formerly lay against the side of the cylinder is inflating, and I can no longer circle the interior.

I'm slowly running out of room. If that membrane reaches me, I won't be able to breathe.

Panic lights a fire inside of me, and I scramble like a sock in a dryer, desperate to escape.

If I can get to that hatch . . .

"Help! Help me!"

A heavy membrane is pressing against my back, and I feel the space shrinking as I scratch toward the opening . . .

WHIRrrrr-rr-r . . . thunk.

The cylinder grinds to a halt, and the air slowly escapes from the other side of the membrane.

The bout of claustrophobia refuses to leave. My heart races, and my breath comes in shallow gasps.

Suddenly, the most wonderful head of blond hair pokes through the hatch — now opening toward the ground — and his citrus-woodsy scent fills the enclosed space.

"Erick! You saved me."

"Always." His hand grips my arm, and he extracts me from the tube of death.

My tears leak onto his comforting flannel shirt as he pulls me tight.

Erick's new priority is discovering who tried to silence me. Fortunately for him, we agree that it's pretty likely that the silencer is the same person who killed Cromwell. So even though I'm insisting we find the killer and he's insisting we find my *attempted* killer, we're on the same page.

"Are you sure you're okay? You don't have to continue. We can report what happened and head home. You look like you could use some french fries." His caring blue eyes hold me in their gaze like Mesmer's.

"To be fair, you and I both know I always look like I could use some fries. I'm not gonna lie, I'm shaken up, but I'm salty enough about someone trying to kill me to want to stick around and find them."

There's a whiff of pride in the air when Erick

slips an arm around me and turns to Nettie. "She might not be able to tackle a linebacker, but she's tough as an old boot."

"Old boot? Rude!" The three of us share a chuckle.

"Tell her what you found, Nettie."

She steps closer, glances over both of her shoulders, and lowers her voice. "Once you guys ruled out JR as a murder suspect, the story about him stealing the grapes didn't quite check out with me. I broke into my father's office—"

"You broke in? Your father kept his office locked? Who was he trying to keep out?" After blurting my questions, I raise both hands apologetically, but Nettie takes pity on me.

"It's a fair question. Now that I know more about how my parents met in France and how my father ran his business, it honestly doesn't surprise me, but I used to wonder the same thing. He would always blame it on spies from other vineyards, or protecting our top-secret viticulture information, even though I kept the notes on all my careful hybridization in an open desk in my office." She rolls her eyes and we both nod.

"I should've realized he had his priorities out of whack, but I guess it never occurred to me."

"Yeah, I get that. Sometimes it's hard for honest people to understand what makes others tick." I'll spare her my knowledge of both sides of the fence and hope that whatever she found helps our investigation.

Nettie nods her agreement to the part I said out loud and continues. "The main thing was, I found the books for the entire operation. There was an entry showing a withdrawal of cash to pay for that shipment of grapes from South America."

Erick steps in. "Was that usual? To pay for a shipment in cash?"

She shakes her head vigorously. "No. Never. There would've been a wire transfer, or at least a bank check. Never cash. The other strange thing about that entire transaction was that after the grapes were theoretically stolen by JR, the cash was never re-deposited."

I whistle softly. "Highly sus-pish."

"I asked Leon what he knew about it this morning, and, rather than answer my question, he furiously defended our father's right to privacy and made me feel like a criminal for breaking into our deceased dad's office."

Chewing the inside of my cheek, I nod slowly. "Classic misdirection. Leon is definitely guilty of something. JR must've jumped in and bought grapes at a discount after Leon failed to pay the shipper. Leon probably needed the money for that wife of his. Whatever it was for, he was involved in embezzling funds. Does that make Leon a murderer?"

"No idea, but it definitely got Erick thinking." Nettie nods to my husband. "We were on our way to the tool room when I heard the grape press running. There's absolutely no way that machine should be on this time of year. As soon as I mentioned that, Erick sprinted as fast as when we had to run fifties back in the day for How-to Fairlane." She grins and nods in appreciation. "I gotta say, he's still got it. The man can move."

I ignore the obvious setup and keep my schoolgirl snickering to myself. "So take me to this tool room. What are we looking for?"

Erick calls the next play. "Nettie and I came to the same conclusion. Whoever sawed the metal bars on that pallet rack must've used a hand tool. A power tool would've caught someone's attention. It may have taken a few days with a hacksaw, but it could've been done at night or on the weekends when there was less chance of other workers wandering around the fermentation room. Anyway, we're looking for a hacksaw."

Nettie leads the way to the well-organized tool room. Pegboard covers an entire wall above a sturdy stainless steel bench. Every tool has its place. The bench has been wiped clean. When Erick opens the cabinet at the end of the bench, it contains only power tools and extension cords.

She points. "There's a hacksaw right there. That blade looks brand-new." Erick removes the saw from the metal hook on the pegboard and inspects it carefully. "Yeah. A little too new, if you ask me."

Suddenly, Pyewacket dragging items from the waste bin for no apparent reason flashes through my memory. "Trash can."

I lunge for the covered trashcan at the end of the workbench, but Erick grabs my arm. "We need to take it slow, Moon. If there's evidence in there, we can't take a chance of destroying it by being over-exuberant and putting our own prints on it."

He glances at the shelving perpendicular to the workbench. "Any latex gloves in there, Nettie?"

She steps forward, grabs us each a pair, and pulls a tarpaulin from the bottom shelf. After carefully spreading it, she and Erick remove the lid from the large trashcan, lay it carefully on the tarp, and the three of us begin the exciting work of trash sorting.

My internal director makes a sarcastic note: insert laugh track here.

The first third of the trashcan will certainly not win any awards for cinematography or surprise. We have a pile of crumpled, blue-paper shop towels, various bits of clear and colored plastic, two caps, and an empty bottle of glue.

Erick lifts the bottom of the can and shakes it lightly to bring us another batch.

As Nettie reaches toward the trashcan, the mood ring on my left hand burns like fire. I glance down and see some kind of narrow blade. "Careful. There's a blade in there."

Erick takes over, expertly using a long screwdriver and a pair of pliers to remove an old rag, about a pound of sawdust, and finally, the pièce de résistance!

He holds it aloft with the pliers. "Here's the old blade from the hacksaw. If they can get some particulate off here that matches the steel pallet racks, that will prove this was used in the planning of the murder, or, even better, if they get a fingerprint, we'll finally be able to nab our killer."

Tears spring unbidden in Nettie's eyes. "There was no love lost between my father and me, but I don't want anyone to get away with murder. And I'm really sorry about what happened to you today, Mitzy. I can't thank you guys enough for literally risking your lives to help me figure this all out."

Erick pats her on the shoulder, and that strange sense of something close to longing floats through the air.

I almost died today. All bets are off. "Nettie, I

know Erick said you weren't into guys, or whatever, but is there something more between the two of you than just a convenient prom date?"

Her mouth lolls open, and her pupils dilate with fear. "What? No, it's just— I never— I'm really sorry we fell out of touch, Erick. You're one of the only people who was genuinely nice to me in high school. A girl who didn't date boys and played football took a lot of flak behind the scenes. You always treated me with respect, and like a friend. I just wish that I'd said thank you back then."

Erick nods and smiles. "I treated you like a friend because you were my friend, Nettie. And you're welcome."

Now I'm blinking back tears — again.

He pulls out his phone, looks at me, and shrugs. "I know this is going to be unpopular, but I have to call Sheriff Paulsen. This is important evidence."

I return his shrug and add a vocalization to match. "Meh. Fine by me. Just please don't tell her someone tried to kill me — again."

He laughs a little too loud. "10-4, Moon. Your secret is safe with me."

The way his eyes drink me in and make so many more promises assures me *all* my secrets are safe.

CHAPTER 25

AFTER A MOMENT OF PONDERING, Erick removes his latex gloves and gazes down. "Let's sit tight and protect the evidence until the sheriff arrives." We all nod our agreement. "It's probably better if you call it in, Nettie."

She bites her lower lip and nods. "I'll pop into the kitchen and make us some sandwiches while we wait. I can multi-task."

"Don't mention what we found to anyone else, Nettie. Whoever killed your father and made the attempt on Mitzy's life needs to feel like they've gotten away with it." Erick's voice carries anger and relief in equal measures.

"Understood. No one will be in the kitchen. I'll just grab some food and be right back."

I maintain my cool until Nettie leaves, but my

stomach is definitely growling. Nothing like a near-death experience to trigger my natural stress eating. Although, to be fair, I tend to eat for a lot of different reasons. Stress is simply part of the plethora of triggers on that list.

Erick continues to stare at the items on the ground in front of us. "I wish I had an evidence bag."

"You don't have an evidence bag?" I press a hand to my chest and widen my gaze in mock horror. "You always seem like the kind of guy who could go on *Let's Make a Deal* and would literally always have an evidence bag. What's up, Harper?"

"That conversation with Alex Crenshaw put me off my game. I'm distracted. Not noticing things I would normally notice. In fact, part of me knew you were in trouble, and it took that comment Nettie made about the grape press to get me running. I can't believe how close I came to losing you — again!"

"Come on. Cut yourself some slack. You're the best detective I know. Even if you're missing a tiny thing here or there, you're still catching more than ninety-five percent of people."

The muscles in his jaw flex, and he glances off to the side. "I don't catch as much as you."

"Hey, where's that coming from? You know my deal. Nobody catches as much as I do. It's not by choice. I'm only trying to do the best I can with whatever this is that I ended up with."

His shoulders sag, and he exhales. "Yeah. I know. And I totally get it. I think I'm having a pity party. That's what you call it, right?"

My laughter is loud and long. "The fact that you don't even know what to call it saddens me, Harper. It's a very clear indication you've never had one."

"Not true. You know I went through some dark days before I found my way to the academy and became sheriff."

"Touché." I'm quick to change the subject. The trauma he suffered in combat is an area I tiptoe around. I can never know what that was like for him. The only thing I can offer is unconditional support and no prying. "You think Paulsen will try to make an arrest when she gets here?"

He shifts his weight and drags a thumb along his jawline. "Probably. Doesn't seem like she'll have a solid suspect until the report comes back on the hacksaw blade, but you know Paulsen. One can never be sure."

I scoff and stare at the blade, hoping against hope there's at least one good print — or anything that ties someone directly to the murder.

Nettie returns with sandwiches and some cider for each of us. "Paulsen was patrolling on the other side of Little Webb Lake. Should be here in like five minutes."

Arching an eyebrow, I glance toward my partner. "Coincidence? I think not. Seems like she might be following us. Her investigation is going nowhere, so she's riding our coattails. I have half a mind—"

"Easy, Moon." Erick chuckles good-naturedly.

We eat our sandwiches in silence and finish our cider as the sound of sirens fills the air.

Through my full mouth, I quip, "*Guess Who's Coming to Dinner*?"

As the only film-school dropout in the tool room, no one seems to get my joke.

Nettie heads off to greet the sheriff. Erick and I stay to protect the evidence.

Voices draw near. Nettie is explaining what we found.

Sheriff Paulsen stomps into the toolshed, glancing from me to Erick and back again. "You two are just never going to be happy until you've completely ruined every crime scene I have left to investigate."

Sometimes I let Erick take her on. I'm not feeling that generous today. "Look, Paulsen, you wouldn't even be here investigating this crime scene if it weren't for us. Your team seems to have given up. Despite what happened to the pallet rack. Despite the remote control in the forklift. Still seems like you were really leaning toward declaring it all an accident."

Paulsen tightens the grip on her holstered gun, narrows her gaze, and steps toward me.

Now it's time for Erick to jump in. "Hey, it's not about who finds what. It's about arresting a murderer." He points to the hacksaw blade, explains our line of reasoning, and assures the sheriff that no one has touched the evidence.

She jumps on the radio. "Deputy Gilbert, bring a large evidence bag to the toolshed behind the fermentation room. We got a hacksaw blade to take into evidence."

Less than a minute later, Aurélie Pearson walks into the toolshed. "Sheriff Paulsen, I choose to turn myself in. You must know about this large insurance policy on my husband. My reasons are my own. No details. Though I had many." She extends her wrists toward the sheriff.

I don't understand what's going on. No part of what Aurélie Pearson said has any ring of truth.

In the distance, a snowmachine roars to life. Erick and I exchange a knowing glance.

Rather than ask any questions or complicate things, Paulsen steps forward and begins reciting Aurélie's Miranda rights as she slips the handcuffs on the slender woman's wrists.

Erick gestures toward the door with a head nod. "Mitzy and I will get out of your way. Do you need us to come into the station and make a statement?"

The sheriff curls her lip in a snarl. "What do you think?"

Yeesh!

Nettie is overcome with emotion, begging for her mother to tell the truth, so Erick and I slip out without further explanation.

A SNOWMOBILE RIPS BETWEEN TWO sections of the vineyard and disappears into the forest. Erick and I run for the shed and are fortunate to find a second machine.

He throws his hands in the air. "There's no key anywhere!"

Grabbing the screwdriver from a nearby toolbox, I teasingly shove my husband back from the machine. "Step aside, Harper. This is a job for a delinquent."

As I approach the ignition, wielding my screwdriver like a weapon, Erick tugs at my arm. "Stand down, Miss Demeanor. I've actually handled this before. I just got frustrated and couldn't think straight."

Placing my hands in the air as though it's a Wild West holdup, I back away from the sled.

Within seconds, he has flipped the hood up, disconnected a wire, and pulled the manual start rope.

We jump on and roar off in pursuit of the man we believe to be Leon.

The snow is flying by, and, as we approach the woods, fear grips me. I've never raced a snowmachine through the woods before.

To be clear, I haven't actually raced a snowmobile anywhere. Just because my father is a champion snowmachine driver doesn't necessarily mean the skill trickled down. Before my last ride home with Erick, the only time I was on a snowmobile for any real length of time was as a captive. But that's another story.

Erick expertly dives into the forest, following the trail of our prey.

Whoever we're after must've been alerted to our pursuit. The tracks begin to zigzag in between the trees.

We follow, and I squeeze my arms more tightly around his waist. The last thing I want to do is fall off this thing and ruin the chase.

Erick fires up the headlight as the oak trees give way to thick pine.

If I close my eyes and focus. I can hear the snowmachine ahead of us.

We're gaining on them.

We take a sharp right. Erick shouts over his shoulder. "He's heading for the lake."

Dear Lord baby Jesus! Please let that lake still be frozen solid!

Bursting from the trees, Erick increases our speed. The sled ahead of us is ripping full throttle toward the wide-open spaces of, I'm assuming, Little Webb Lake.

Just as we get within a hundred easy yards of our quarry, Erick eases off the throttle and steers left.

"What are you doing? We almost have him!"

Rather than giving it more gas, Erick comes to a stop. He flips a clip on the handlebar to engage the brake, jumps from the sled, and pulls me from the seat.

He clicks the latch and angles the seat open, grabbing a coiled tow strap from the storage compartment.

Before I can ask any follow-up questions, there's an eerie, high-pitched creak followed by a bone-chilling crack.

The sled and rider, attempting to escape, crash through the ice.

CHAPTER 26

THINGS ARE RACING before my eyes! Erick moves like a perfectly tuned machine.

Meanwhile, my feet are frozen in place as I watch in horror.

The sled we were chasing is sinking fast, and the driver, who all my extra senses confirm is Leon Pearson, scrambles to escape.

Something's wrong.

He rips off his helmet, throws it onto the ice, and shouts in panic. "Help me! I'm stuck!"

Another terrifying crack knifes through the silence, and the sled is gone. Erick flips one end of the tow strap around something on our snowmachine, ties the other end around his waist, and crawls on his belly toward the widening cleft in the ice.

Leon screams and splashes. The weight of the sinking snowmobile is pulling him down.

"Take a deep breath, Leon. Dive under and try to free your leg." Erick's voice is loud, commanding, but most of all, calm.

He's still two body lengths from the opening when Leon's head submerges.

It does not resurface.

Erick calls over his shoulder. "Call the station. Tell them to get Paulsen and the ice rescue team out here ASAP."

This has to be the first time in my life I've wanted to see Sheriff Paulsen.

I rip off my mitten, and the cold bites into my flesh as I tap the number for the station. In the middle of my explanation of events and repetition of Erick's command, a scream rips from my throat. "No!"

All that's left on the ice are Erick's jacket and snow boots.

He somehow wriggled out of them and dove through that icy hole.

The voice on the other end of the phone attempts to calm me.

"I don't know what's happening. Erick just dove in after him. You guys have to get out here. I don't know what to do. I grew up in the desert!"

Deputy Baird promises to stay on the phone

with me until help arrives.

My instinct is to walk closer and offer assistance.

She must hear my footsteps crunching in the crust of snow on the lake, or possibly it's a guess at what I might do.

Baird tells me in no uncertain terms that the worst possible thing I can do is walk closer to the break in the ice.

Apparently, more sections could break off at any moment. The safest thing for me to do is to stay where I'm at. She tells me to check the snowmachine for any kind of first aid gear or a thermal blanket.

Tapping the speaker icon, I search the sled. All I can think about is the fact that Erick hasn't come up for air.

A staccato stuttering in the sky above me draws my attention.

Baird must hear it, too. "That's the rescue squad. They should be landing any minute. Don't panic. Stay where you are. They'll handle everything."

"How long can someone hold their breath?" My voice is shaky and I can't swallow.

Deputy Baird does her best to assure me that Erick is in tip-top shape and he'll be popping out of that hole any minute.

Two men jog across the ice. One carries the medical gear, and the other a backboard and rescue rope. When they reach me, they drop the medical gear, attach one end of the rope to the backboard and secure the other end to the sled. Now, the first man flat crawls toward the opening, pushing the bright yellow body-sized board ahead of him.

His progress is horrifyingly slow! The other man preps their gear. He spreads a thermal blanket on the ice, sets out a portable defibrillator — I've seen them on television — and several sealed syringes. It doesn't look good.

Rescuer number one is about a body length from the opening when my personal ice merman breaks through the surface. "I've got him. Chuck, give me a rope."

Rescuer number one must be "Chuck." He uncoils a length of rope secured to the backboard and tosses it. Erick takes the looped end and dives below the surface for the second time.

Tears are forming icicles on my eyelashes. I can't remember the last time I took a breath.

Erick reappears and begins feeding the snared, limp body of Leon Pearson to Chuck.

Chuck skillfully pulls Leon onto the board and backs away from the hole in the ice, dragging Pearson with him, keeping his weight spread out and staying low.

When he reaches the halfway point, he calls for his buddy. Together they drag Napoleon to the triage area, untie the rope from Leon, and begin work.

Erick's lips are bluish-purple, and his hands have no color at all. His attempts to climb onto the ice are failing. The moment he gets any traction, another chunk of ice gives way beneath him.

I turn to seek help and trip over the tow strap linking Erick to the snowmachine. The hook flips loose and whips across the ice like a rogue grocery cart.

"Chuck! I knocked the strap loose! Erick can't get out."

The ice-rescue pro returns with his looped rope and begins creeping forward.

Chuck lassoes Erick like a baby calf and gets the rope under his arms.

My lungs feel as though they might explode. I gasp for breath.

Finally, Erick is on the unstable ice, shaking like an autumn leaf in a windstorm, and Chuck is coaxing him toward solid ice.

I feel utterly helpless. When my husband finally reaches safety, he rolls out of the rope and doesn't move. His breathing is so shallow I almost can't hear it.

Without thinking, I hurry toward his discarded coat and boots.

Chuck shouts for me to stop.

All I can think of is that my guy needs to be kept warm.

Grabbing the coat and boots, I turn and feel the ice giving way.

Call it psychic ability, call it innate alchemy, call it dumb luck. Somehow, I throw myself forward and land on solid ice.

Crawling to Erick, I push the boots on his feet and try to get the coat underneath him.

The medic helps load Erick onto the snowmachine. "Can you drive him to the helo?"

"Drive? The snowmobile?" There isn't an ounce of confidence in my voice.

He points to various apparatuses on the sled and gives me a thirty-second lesson. "Just aim her toward the helicopter. We'll carry the other man. What did you say his name was?"

"That's Napoleon Pearson."

"Well, we have room for four in the helo. We'll take them directly to the hospital, and you can meet us there. You're okay to drive this sled back to the winery, right?"

I am absolutely not okay to drive the sled anywhere, but getting Erick to the hospital is my top priority. "Yeah, sure."

Turning the skis toward the shore, I squeeze the gas and lurch forward. Erick begins to fall away, and I have to grab his jacket with my free hand.

The two rescuers have Napoleon on the backboard-turned-stretcher and are running at an impressive clip toward the helicopter.

Holding Erick's parka firmly with one hand, I attempt to drive a snowmachine — for the first time in my life — with only my right hand.

I wouldn't win any awards, and I'm sure my dad would have more than one pointer to offer, but I get there. My human snowman of a husband is convulsing with shivers.

Chuck grips Erick like he's a simple bag of groceries and loads him into the helicopter.

He takes one look at me, gives me a thumbs up and points to his left. "That way back to the winery. You're doing great."

The helicopter lifts off, dusting me and everything around in a fine powder of snow.

As soon as the stuttering whir of the blades vanishes, the waterworks turn on full blast.

Driving a snowmobile toward a location you're unsure of, while sobbing uncontrollably, is a pretty terrible combination.

Stopping the sled, I scrape my icy tears away with my mittens and take several deep breaths. I have to focus and let my extra senses guide me back to the winery. Good ol' Mitzy Moon was definitely not paying attention when Erick darted through the forest in pursuit of Leon.

Trusting in my psychic abilities, I eventually find my way back to Châteauneuf-du-Nord and run through the rear entrance, desperate to find Nettie.

The pressing room and the fermentation room are empty. As I approach the tasting room, muffled sobs draw me in.

Nettie is seated at a table next to a half-empty bottle of wine and a stack of tear-soaked napkins.

"Nettie? Mind if I join you?" She looks in my direction and exhales a ragged breath. "Was it Leon? On the snowmobile?"

"It was."

"Did he confess?"

After bringing her up to speed on the terrifying events on Webb Lake, Nettie pours me a glass of wine. "Will you join me?"

"I wish I could, but I have to get to the hospital. Do you want to join *me*?"

She shakes her head viciously. "Not a chance. If Leon did this, and I feel certain that he did, I have no interest in looking at a man who would let his mother take the fall for his wickedness."

Driving back to Pin Cherry, I hold one image clear in my mind. Erick. Breathing and alive. That's the only thing that matters now.

CHAPTER 27

On the snowy drive to the hospital, my heart wants me to race 120 miles per hour, but fortunately my head prevails, and I drive at a reasonable speed for the treacherous winter conditions.

The helicopter is still on the pad when I arrive at the Birch County Regional Medical Center. For a moment I worry, then an inner voice assures me it's a good thing no one else needs to be rescued today.

Parking near the emergency entrance, I rush inside.

The nurse at the desk looks up calmly. "How can I help you, miss?"

Yeesh! You'd think she does this all day. Oh, wait—

"The helicopter brought in my boyfriend — I mean, husband — Erick Harper. Can I see him?"

She smiles and gets to her feet. "Let me take you to him, dear."

The nurse walks past several rooms full of patients. She pushes through the double doors into the emergency room proper and passes a number of beds with curtains drawn around them like individual waterless shower stalls.

Raised voices, laughter, and general hilarity reach my ears before we turn the corner.

Sitting on a gurney in the hallway, with his feet in some sort of heated boot contraption, and a blanket wrapped around his loosely tied hospital gown, my husband is holding court.

The two men from the helicopter rescue team, four paramedics, two nurses, and a man who is either a surgeon fresh out of the theater or a lost butcher in medical scrubs, are all held in Erick's thrall.

"His boot got sucked into the track and pulled his whole leg in — up to his knee! It was insane. Never seen anything like it. I had to get his foot out of the boot, but I wasn't sure if the sprocket had pierced the skin, you know?"

His rapt audience nods and murmurs their understanding.

"The whole time I was working on that boot,

the sled was pulling us deeper and deeper. Man, that water is cold!"

Chuck pipes up. "You betcha. We had a rescue over on Island Lake last week. My heart about stopped when I went under. And I was wearing a thermal wetsuit." He points both hands at Erick and glances at the gathered crowd. "This guy was wearing jeans and a T-shirt!" The crowd laughs uproariously, and a couple paramedics pat Erick firmly on the back.

Then he catches sight of me.

"Mitzy!" He tries to jump from the bed, but brawny arms restrain him.

I strut forward, kick out one hip, and plant my fist firmly on my curves. "And here I was, all worried about you, sweetie. Should I order pizza for you and your friends?"

The entire group laughs uproariously and tries to outdo each other, complimenting my husband.

He pulls me close, kisses my cheek, and smiles. "Hey, I wasn't the only hero out there today. This one ran back to the hole in the ice, got my boots and jacket, and jumped free when a huge section broke loose."

Gasps and cheers abound.

Stepping up to the plate, I toot my own horn or pitch my own home run — it's a mixed metaphor. "That was nothing. I've never driven a snowmachine before in my life, and I had to drive one all the way back to Châteauneuf-du-Nord. Not to mention, I had no idea where it was!"

Chuck pats me on the back. "You did great, Mrs. Harper."

Erick holds up a finger and shakes it firmly in Chuck's direction. "That's Mrs. Moon, sir. Thanks again for the assist out there. Any word on Leon?"

The man in blood-spattered scrubs nods. "They're closing him up now. We were able to get his heart going with an open cardiac massage, and he'll be in the hospital for at least a week. Fortunately, the cold water slowed his breathing and heart rate, which bought him some time. We think he was possibly only without oxygen for five minutes or less. We'll know more when he's conscious."

Erick nods. "I can't believe Leon drove onto that dark patch of ice. He's lived here his whole life. He should've recognized the danger signs."

The group nods solemnly and disperses.

Chuck hangs back and grips Erick's hand for one final shake. "We sure do miss you out there, Sheriff. I know you're not the sheriff anymore. But I'm just saying . . ."

As though the mere mention of the title could summon her, Paulsen waddles around the corner. "I'm gonna need statements from both of you. Why the hell were you chasing Leon Pearson across a frozen lake?"

Placing my hand on Erick's knee, I squeeze – hard. "Oh, I guess we were a step ahead of you – again. Leon Pearson killed his father."

Paulsen's right hand rests, as usual, on her holstered gun, and she shakes her head in fierce disagreement. "Wrong again, amateur. The wife already copped to the murder. She had a five-million-dollar life insurance policy on Cromwell. Her and her brother were planning to escape to France before I got a hold of them."

Erick looks at me, winks, and lies back on the gurney.

Time for me to take the current sheriff down a peg.

"Oh, is that so, Paulsen? I think you might have a few of your facts confused. We're the ones who told Aurélie about the insurance policy. She had no idea. I'm sure if you look into it, you'll discover Cromwell took the policy out on himself and named her as the beneficiary."

She shrugs.

"And if you follow up on that supposed theft of grapes from South America, I think you'll also find that Leon Pearson embezzled that money from the winery and never paid the suppliers. He has a mountain of debt. Sure, he stood to inherit, but not soon enough. His wife's spending habits, combined with his clashing viewpoints regarding winemaking, pushed him over the edge. He's the only one with the skill necessary to rig up the remote control on the forklift, tamper with the high-tech digital thermostat, and attempt to dispose of the evidence."

"What evidence? We found the receiver."

"But you never found the transmitter. And, technically, you didn't find the hacksaw blade either. That was us. Harper and Moon Investigations." I pause to point to myself and Erick. "Our statement is that we were pursuing a murderer who fled the scene of a crime. And then my bighearted husband rescued him from drowning when his sled broke through the ice."

Paulsen's mouth works like a fish out of water, but no sound emerges.

"So, I think that about wraps it up. As usual, it was a pleasure doing business with you, Sheriff." I make no attempt to hide the snark in my tone as I utter her title.

"We'll see if any of your story checks out when Napoleon Pearson regains consciousness."

"Be my guest. But try to remember that the only reason Napoleon Pearson will be regaining consciousness is due to the heroic efforts of former Sheriff Erick Harper."

Paulsen turns and stomps toward the exit,

mumbling something about amateurs under her breath.

Turning my full attention to my husband, I gaze into his twinkling blue eyes. "You made a right hero out of yourself today, Harper."

He fusses with his IV line and finally gets it out of the way. Then pulls me close. "We make a good team, Moon. Thanks for having my back out there."

Snuggling into his neck, I whisper, "I always have your back, Harper." Dragging my fingers across the planes of his chest, I add, "And sometimes your front."

Throaty laughter fills the hallway, and I can't wait to get home and tell Grams—

Blerg. I guess it's more of a "one problem solved, one to go" situation.

CHAPTER 28

When Erick and I drive past the Bell, Book & Candle to turn down the alley, I'm surprised to see the enormous chandelier above the stacks still glowing.

We enter through the walk-up and find that, once again, Pyewacket has strewn trash throughout the open-plan kitchen.

The furry fiend is nowhere to be seen.

I march toward the door separating our home from the bookshop, but Erick grabs my arm and pulls my body behind his. "We don't know who's out there. If it turns out that Artemis Ward has already found us, I'll be the one to face her."

As I open my mouth to protest, a screech erupts from my throat, and I stumble backward, clutching my chest.

My husband lunges toward me with concern. "What happened? Is she doing something to you?"

Waving my hands, I suck in air and exhale loudly. "The amulet. The pendant that Silas gave me. It started talking to me. It's never happened before, so—"

He heaves a sigh of relief. "Okay. What's your necklace telling you?" Erick lifts both of his hands in the air and stares helplessly.

"Thanks for not calling me a freak. Silas is here. In spite of his idea of keeping his distance from me, there was a book in the Loft that he had to have." Swinging the clear quartz pendant between my fingers, I add, "This thingy says there's good news."

Erick smiles. "That's great. Let's go hear the good news. We could definitely use some."

He pulls the door open for me, and I hurry through. Not wanting to tempt fate any further today, I unhook the "No Admittance" chain, and Erick clips it in place behind us.

Hustling up the steps, I shout, "Silas? You said you had good news."

A solid harrumph echoes off the tin-plated ceiling, and, when I reach the top of the circular staircase, my mentor is still smoothing his bushy grey mustache with a thumb and forefinger.

Before he can comment, the tan terror curled beside him rises.

Pyewacket arches his back in a pose I like to call Halloween cat, and saunters toward me with an unblinking gaze.

"Yes, your highness, you were right about everything, as usual. So you can stop dragging the trash all over the kitchen. We found the hacksaw blade in the waste bin in the tool room. All hail Robin Pyewacket Goodfellow."

With an irritated flick of his tail, he lifts his chin and sits directly at my feet.

Bending, I scratch between his black-tufted ears and coo additional praise.

"Oh, Silas, BTW, we need to make a donation to Artie's snowplow memorial fund — or whatever she calls it. All right?"

He glances toward me briefly and his jowls waggle in acknowledgment. Clearly that's all I'm getting on that topic right now.

Erick places two chairs opposite the oak reading table where Silas has opened a deep-oxblood leather-bound book on a wooden stand. He wears a pair of Twiggy's special white gloves. We sit opposite him.

"This looks serious, Silas. How old is that book?"

He steeples his fingers and bounces his jowly chin on the tip of his gloved pointers.

Right. A lesson.

Reaching out with my extrasensory perceptions, I use a technique called psychometry. However, with a special Mitzy Moon twist. Silas taught me how to get images and impressions from an object without having to physically touch it. "All right, the book was published in 1505. And the title is *Tractatulus Hypocratis* by an Italian philosopher."

My mentor ceases his nodding and smiles. "Excellent, Mizithra. You have earned this wonderful news."

Leaning forward too eagerly, I nearly touch the book.

Silas swats my hand away and scowls. "Calm down. I shall share my news presently."

Leaning back in my seat like a child waiting outside a principal's office — which I've done — I tap my foot impatiently.

"Your grandmother's situation is unique. In all the world, I'm certain there are other ghosts who enjoy her privilege. However, I am not privy to any of those spirits. I have compiled a plethora of information about this 'in between' space in which Myrtle Isadora now resides." He pauses and sighs. "Something is pulling her through the veil. Or, rather, pushing her."

"What? What's pushing her? It's not me. I want her here more than anything." My tone is anxious and my interruption not appreciated.

He harrumphs. "The Egyptians buried their dead with many items meant to aid them in their journey, and perhaps even serve them in the afterlife. Your grandmother chose her favorite gown, her favorite shoes, and many pieces of her beloved jewelry."

I'm terrible at this. I can't control myself. "Are you saying that the piece of her dress and the left shoe she lost in that séance gone wrong are pulling her through the veil?"

He clears his throat and fixes me with a disheartened glare. "I am not. What I intended to share is that there was an item that held great power, perhaps the greatest power in any realm, that was missing when your grandmother's casket was placed in the ground."

Pressing my lips together, I struggle to hold my tongue. Instead, I raise both of my hands and shake them in the air in frustration.

Erick slips an arm around my shoulder and attempts to share some of his calm patience with me.

Silas smiles appreciatively at my husband and continues. "You are an apt pupil, Mizithra. You've learned far more than many of the pupils I have ever had in my tutelage. What power do you believe to be the greatest above and below?" He gestures to the heavens and the earth.

My stymied brain begins to spin off in the

wrong direction, but I catch myself and breathe deeply. "Love. It has to be love."

"Indeed." He crosses his arms and leans back in his chair.

Clearly he expects me to crack this whole fading ghost mystery with one—

"The ring!" I wave my right hand frantically. "The wedding ring Odell gave her. Her one true love. The ring she had sewn in her coat. The one thing she—" Tears fill my eyes and swallow my words.

Silas carefully closes the great tome and returns it with reverence to its spot on the shelf. He removes his white gloves, drops them in a small basket, and places the bookstand beside it. Then he returns to his chair and smiles so wide it lifts his heavy jowls. "This emptiness is weakening your grandmother's spirit. The love that is imbued in that ring could hold her spirit on this side of the veil. If only she could possess it."

"But we can't give her anything. Lord knows I've tried to give that woman a handkerchief plenty of times. She can move things in the physical plane, but they don't become part of her ghost. This is hopeless!"

Erick rubs my shoulder and leans forward. "I'm way out of my depth here, Silas, so feel free to tell me I'm crazy, but it kinda sounds like you're saying we need to put this ring on Isadora's finger."

The milky film in my mentor's eyes vanishes, and the powerful alchemist that hides within sparks to life. "If ever there were a perfect protector, Mr. Harper, you are he."

"Can somebody please tell me what's going on? I just explained we can't give Grams any—" My mouth falls open and the words evaporate. Are they saying what I think they're saying? Oh, I think I'm gonna be sick.

Silas takes one look at my green-around-the-gills face and sighs. "We must exhume your grandmother. And that ring must be placed on her finger. There is an incantation that should be recited at the right moment, but I believe this will heal her. This will return her to us."

My hand goes to my throat, and I struggle to swallow. "I can't. I can't do it, Silas."

"You would keep the ring from your grandmother?"

"No. Never. She can have the ring. That's not what I'm saying. I can't— Her corpse will be— I can't see her skeleton!"

Silas rises from his chair and walks calmly toward me. He places a hand on my shoulder, and I immediately feel grounding energy coursing through my body.

"This is not a task for you. If it were, I know you would find the strength to complete it. You have faced worse, with less."

"Silas, I know I said I would do anything for Grams, and I would. But — is there some kind of potion I can drink?"

He narrows his gaze.

"I don't mean a magical potion. That's not what I meant. Like a tincture, or what's the other word? Decoction?" The flow of words ceases, and my brain finally processes what Silas said. "If I'm not the one who has to do this, then who?"

He finally allows himself a light chuckle. "Perhaps you can speak to your grandfather. We are all in uncharted waters here, Mizithra. It is my belief that if the ring were to be placed by the object of her affection, by the man who imbued the token with its original love, it would perhaps have the most power."

"So, I don't have to do it? I just have to get Odell to do it? No problem. He will totally be on board."

Silas nods, and Erick leans forward. "I'm not trying to be negative, Mr. Willoughby, but you and I both know digging graves in the winter at this latitude is unheard of. Bodies are placed in cold storage and the graves are created later, after the frozen earth thaws. The way you two are talking, it doesn't sound like we have that kind of time."

The mood ring on my left hand burns at the same moment Pyewacket offers a ferocious vocalization.

"R-OW!"

"I haven't heard that one before, and I don't know what it means, but I will be right back." Bolting from the chair, I race down the stairs and risk jumping over the chain.

Success!

Continuing my sprint, I blast through the "Employees Only" door into the kitchen. Falling to my knees, I rifle through the mess of trash left by my furry overlord and find what I'm looking for.

Racing back to the Rare Books Loft with the paper held higher than an Olympic torch, I stop and wave the sheet. I'm disappointed when Erick and Silas fail to cheer. "Do you know what this is?"

Silas harrumphs. "We most certainly do not."

"It's a flyer that came in the mail for *winter* excavating. These guys can dig up Grams."

CHAPTER 29

Before Operation Excavation can get underway, Erick's phone rings with a call from Nettie. He passes the phone to me, takes the winter excavation flyer, and offers me a wink.

Thank goodness! I had no idea how to explain my cemetery-based winter excavation needs to a man named Frisby.

"Hey, Nettie, it's Mitzy. Erick is handling some business. Is there something I can help you with?"

In the background, my husband is leaving a message for the company. He ends the call and gestures for me to put Nettie Pearson on speaker.

"Sorry to interrupt. Erick is back. I'm putting you on speaker. Can you repeat what you were saying?"

Nettie obliges. "Hey, my dad's — well, I guess

he's *my* lawyer now. Anyway, the lawyer called. He's been in communication with Paulsen on this entire investigation. You'll be happy to hear that once Leon was faced with our mother going to prison for his crimes, he made a full confession. The lawyer said there was a clause in my father's will specifically stating that if any of his children were found responsible for his death, they would be disinherited and their portion of the estate divided between the remaining offspring."

"Congratulations! I mean, I know that sounds weird." Shrugging my shoulders at Erick, I hope he can help me extract my foot from my mouth.

"What Mrs. Moon is trying to say, Nettie, is that despite the terrible circumstances, the winery has finally landed in the right hands. You can work with Manny, right?"

"Yeah. They released him, too. He wasn't running from the law or anything. He had a longstanding appointment with an interior designer in New York. He was simply on his way to take care of some business related to the hotel he wants to open. He claims it didn't dawn on him that he shouldn't leave the state."

Erick inhales sharply. "I have to say, I tend to believe him. I've honestly heard the same thing from suspects before."

They're skipping all the good stuff, and it's really bugging me. "Nettie, if you and Manny inherit the winery equally, then will you have a fifty percent share in the hotel?"

"Yeah. Manny and I will work out the details. But we want the same things. We want to protect the winery, keep the family winemaking techniques, and make this a destination. You know, for weddings, family reunions, anniversaries — all of that."

Erick and I respond in unison. "That's great news."

We exchange an "uh oh" glance, and I stifle a giggle.

Nettie takes a deep breath. "I can't thank you guys enough. I would've lost everything if it wasn't for you helping—" Emotion chokes off her voice, and Erick jumps in.

"Hey, just a friend doing another friend a favor. This friend is going to be sending you an invoice, but you know what I mean." His wry humor does the trick, and Nettie laughs away her tears.

"Oh, and Uncle P talked my mom into staying. He has to undergo at least two more surgeries, and they told him it will be six months of physical therapy at a minimum. He wants to do it here. He wants to stay on as the winemaker for as long as he can."

"Is your mother all right with that?" Based on

Aurélie's reaction to returning to France, I'm concerned she's once again giving up agency in her own life.

"Mom and I had a long talk — in French. She said her reasons for returning were mostly about escape and leaving behind all the pain of her arranged marriage to my father. Now that he's out of the picture, and Manny and I will be running everything, she's looking forward to seeing the winery become what she always envisioned. She said it's starting to feel like her winery now. And I kind of love that for her."

Now tears are forming in my eyes, and Erick slips his arm around my shoulders.

"Look, Pearson, you let Mitzy and I know when you're having the grand reopening. We want front-row seats. And I hope you never have to hire us again."

Nettie breathes an enormous sigh of relief and inhales a ragged breath. "Yeah. You guys are amazing, but you know that."

Erick kisses my forehead, and I exhale loudly. "Oh, trust me. We know. All the best to you and your family."

"Same to you guys, and thanks again." Nettie ends the call.

My husband hugs me and turns to leave, but I have a burning question. "Um, what do you think will happen with Kylah once Leon goes to prison?"

He tilts his head from one shoulder to the other. "I hate to take bets on someone's marriage. Seems like bad karma, but I give it six months. I say she divorces him, tries to get some kind of settlement from the estate, and re-marries an older, wealthier man within the year."

Doing my best "JR" imitation, I lean away and hunch my shoulders. "That's harsh, bruh."

Erick laughs, I giggle, and Pyewacket yowls loud enough to wake the dead.

Oops. I guess we do have some urgent business to attend to.

Cut to —

A stout man with a massive sledgehammer and several steel rods.

He bashes steel rods into the ground at least four feet deep, then connects all the rods with thick wire which ties into a generator. Odell, Erick, Silas, and I watch with a mixture of shock and horror.

If you've seen the original *Frankenstein* movie, you would be as creeped out as me. There's something about the charge of electricity running through the wires encircling a grave that calls to mind the awakening of a monster.

Not that Grams is a monster! Not in the slightest. It's just a weird visual. Odell slips an arm around me and whispers, "If I didn't believe Silas to be a straight shooter, I might think this whole thing was an elaborate prank. You really think this heatin' up the ground idea is gonna help them dig up Myrtle Isadora?"

"Your guess is as good as mine, Gramps. I know exactly nothing about winter excavating."

He chuckles and returns his gaze to the bizarre operation at the cemetery.

Thick snow covers the slopes and flats of the large, oddly picturesque graveyard. The drapery of winter hides the details of lost loved ones under a hushed blanket. It's a relief that we're alone in the cemetery, tending to our strange business without the prying eyes of other heartbroken families.

Fortunately, Erick's former connections helped us push through an exhumation order in record time. Silas created an impressive legal description of why a DNA sample was required to verify the authenticity of my inheritance.

In fact, it was so believable, I began to worry I might be exposed as a fraud. Then I remembered we're not actually taking a DNA sample, and I started to calm down.

Frisby, the owner of the aforementioned winter excavation company, takes several temperature readings of the soil. Then he hops into a mini excavator and precisely places his shovel inside the perimeter.

To the surprise of the three men accompanying me, the scoop sinks into the earth with ease. In about fifteen minutes, we've uncovered a coffin.

This is the part where I step back and convince myself not to toss my cookies. Or, in this case, it would be my chorizo and eggs, since we came to the graveyard straight after breakfast.

Yet another phrase I never imagined saying in my lifetime!

Once the last of the debris is hand-cleared, Frisby retrieves his steel bars and wiring. Next he feeds thick webbed straps under the coffin, and slowly cranks my grandmother's supposedly final resting place from the earth.

Odell squeezes my hand and whispers, "I'll need that ring, kid."

"Oh, right." Pulling off my mitten, I wiggle the precious ring, with its tiny flake of diamond, from my right hand.

As I reach toward Odell's palm, the straps that suspend the coffin jam and it lists dangerously.

I gasp and drop the ring.

"Oh my gosh! I dropped the ring! I'll never find it in this snow!"

Panic overtakes me, and every one of my special abilities shuts down.

Erick walks around the gaping hole in the ground, calmly crouches in front of me, and pulls the ring from the knee-deep snow.

"What the—?"

He smiles up at me. "Um, I've met you. As soon as you pulled your mitten off, I knew you'd drop the ring. I simply kept my eye on its landing place and remained calm."

"Touché." I'm both miffed and relieved. Mostly relieved.

Erick hands the ring to Odell, and Odell grips Erick's hand and pulls him to his feet.

Frisby has successfully pulled the coffin to the surface, and Silas steps forward to open the lid. "Thank you for your assistance, Frisby. Would you mind waiting at the bottom of the hill? Out of respect for the family."

He adjusts the flaps on his deer stalker hat and nods solemnly. "You betcha. Let me know when you're ready to lower her back down."

"Indeed we shall."

Our excavator trudges off through the snow, and Silas turns to address the three of us. "Odell, as you place the ring on her finger — and, if memory serves, the ring finger on her left hand is vacant — you must recite this phrase: Amor aeternus."

Odell clears his throat and nods. "Amor aeternus. Did I get it right?"

Silas offers a weak smile. "Your pronunciation is satisfactory. We shall remain silent as you perform the ritual."

Erick and I step back.

My mentor approaches Odell and places a hand on his shoulder. "You must envision her as she once was. On the day you gave her that ring. What lies within this coffin is not the woman you love. She resides in your mind. You see the woman to whom you made your vows. That is the Myrtle Isadora to whom you make this pledge. That is the hand that accepts the ring."

A strange glistening emanates from Odell's eyes, and he turns almost robotically to the coffin.

Silas adjusts a catch and carefully opens the lid. I look away before any unseemly image of what the coffin contains can ruin my memories of Ghost-ma.

I hold her shimmering face in my heart and let the memory of her voice and her tinkling laughter flood over me.

Odell murmurs, "You are as beautiful as the first day I laid eyes on you, Myrtle."

Silas must have used some alchemy to bend reality and shift Odell's vision. There's no way the contents of that coffin look anything like a twenty-something Myrtle Isadora!

My grandfather recites the special incantation with perfection, and Erick whispers softly, "It's okay, Moon. It's done. They closed the lid."

Silas signals to Frisby, and, in minutes, the coffin is lowered and the soil replaced.

The excavator loads up his gear, shakes my mentor's hand, and carefully drives his one-man machine toward the waiting flatbed in the cemetery parking lot.

Stepping forward, I touch the stone cardinal I placed on Isadora's headstone years ago and brush the snow from his icy back. *Grams, if you can hear me, we need you at the Bell, Book & Candle. I need you every day. This isn't your final resting place. This is simply a place for people who barely knew you to experience remembrance. Those of us who love you most will be waiting for you in the bookshop.*

When I turn away from the headstone, Silas, Erick, and Odell have all bowed their heads. Even though I spoke my prayer in silence, they seemed to know how sacred the moment was to me.

Grasping hands with my amazing husband, we trudge through the deep snow, holding a respectful silence as we pass the headstones of long-lost mothers, fathers, brothers, sisters, and children. I nod my head solemnly as we pass the memorial stones of my stepbrother's parents.

There's a heavy sadness in my heart, and I can only hope it's for those who've crossed over and not the permanent loss of my dear grandmother.

Finally, we all arrive back at the Jeep, and Erick ferries us to the bookstore on Main Street.

Odell kisses me on the cheek. "You'll let me know what happens, right?"

"You'll be my first call, Gramps."

He smiles and marches off toward the diner.

Silas harrumphs. "I had hoped to spend the night here, but I'm experiencing deep unease. I fear I must take my leave and maintain my distance, as we previously discussed. You have the amulet, Mizithra. And you know how it works."

Throwing my arms around his neck, I kiss his jowly cheek. "Thank you. Thank you for everything. I know you'll find a way to stop Artemis Ward. I believe in you."

He leans back, and a single tear trickles down his cheek and disappears into his thick mustache. "And I, you."

He departs as I attempt to convince Erick we have to sleep in the apartment.

"She can't even get into the walk-up at full strength. The sigils that Silas put up to protect our privacy and keep her out will prevent her from letting me know she's back safe. Plus, I'm not gonna be able to sleep regardless of where we crash. So, I pick here, and I totally understand if you'd rather go back to the walk-up."

He circles his arms around my waist. "And miss the very best Valentine's Day surprise of my life? Nothing could make me happier than seeing your face *when* your grandmother returns.

Tears flow from my eyes and I choke out the words, "Yeah, when — not if."

CHAPTER 30

Erick sleeps soundly beside me on the antique four-poster bed.

Pyewacket and I are snuggled together under the thick down comforter, scanning the room for any sign of my grandmother's reappearance.

Moonlight filters through the 6 x 6 windows facing the great lake, and the world lies silent. Hushed under the blanket of fresh snow.

What if it wasn't enough? What if we can't bring her back and anchor her on this side of the veil? What will I do without her?

Pyewacket stirs beside me, and his tall ears twitch.

"What is it? Grams? Grams, are you here?"

My exuberant outburst rouses my husband.

"Do you see her?" He yawns and rubs my leg with one sleepy hand.

"No. I don't see anything yet. But Pyewacket was acting weird."

The silver moonlight illuminates the chiseled jaw next to me as he offers reassurance. "They say animals can sense the presence of a ghost even when people can't see them."

"What? Since when did you become an expert on spirits?"

He scoots closer and lovingly drags his fingers down my arm. "Ever since I met this really hot chick who has special powers, I started researching the supernatural."

His playful teasing brightens my mood. I exhale softly. "Maybe you're right. Maybe all your love-struck research is onto something." Turning to my mystical caracal, I ask the obvious question. "Pye, is Grams back?"

"Reow." Can confirm.

My heart races with excitement, and I leap from the bed.

I mean, I attempt to leap from the bed. My feet get wadded up in the bedding, and I roll hooves over horns onto the carpet.

Somewhere in the ether, the soft, tinkling laughter of Myrtle Isadora echoes.

"Grams! Please tell me this is not my imagination. It's really you, right?"

Standing perfectly still, I take a single deep breath and focus every extrasensory perception I possess on being here, now.

A flutter of something in front of the window catches my attention. It's only a strange wiggling blur, like heat rising off a paved road in the Arizona desert, but it's enough.

"Grams! I can see you." Rushing to the spot where I clocked the visual disturbance, Ghost-ma's energy surrounds me. "She's here! She's here! Text Odell."

"Sweetie, it's after two in the morning. Are you sure?"

A whisper that I almost seem to imagine says, "Tell Odell."

"Yes! Do it. Grams says to do it."

Erick fires off a text, and, seconds later, gets a response.

"Odell says he'll ask Tally and her daughter to run the diner in the morning. He'll bring us breakfast. How early is too early?"

Spinning around like a B-list actress in the rain, I reply through a face-splitting grin. "There's no way I'm going to sleep! He can come whenever he wants."

Erick relays the message and snuggles against the pillow. "You should let Silas know."

Rather than my phone, I touch the pendant around my neck, shimmering in the moonglow, and attempt to send a message.

Despite my expectations, getting a response shocks me. "It worked. I sent, like, a message or whatever through this crystal. Silas responded."

Now that we've taken care of the most important details, I can bask in the happiness of her return.

"Grams, I can't really see you clearly. Your voice is so quiet. It sounds far away. What can I do?"

Out of nothingness, a single hand appears and, on the left ring finger, is the symbol of love Odell so carefully placed on her hand.

My eyes widen as I gasp. "Erick, it worked. I saw her hand for a minute, and the wedding ring is on her finger!"

A moment later, Ghost-ma appears. Her apparition is still weak and flickering, but I see her from head to toe. The hem of her Marchesa gown is still torn, and she's missing her left Valentino shoe. Who cares? She's back!

"Grams! You're back, baby!"

Pyewacket reows excitedly and races circles around her reemerging ghost.

She wiggles her left hand at me and smiles. "It's perfect! It's exactly what I needed! That Silas Willoughby is a genius."

Before I can offer my agreement, she continues. "Now, I need you to take that teal Oscar de la Renta and the silver Christian Louboutins to my casket right away. Would you be a dear and do that for me?"

Classic Grams. "Look, Myrtle Isadora, digging up coffins is not my new pastime. We managed an emergency exhumation to keep you on this side of the veil. I will not be returning to the cemetery to dig you up every season and update your wardrobe."

"Well, I never!"

I can barely get the words out because my heart is so filled with love. "I think we both know that's not true, Myrtle Isadora Johnson Linder Duncan Willamet Rogers."

Soft snoring from the king-sized bed indicates Erick is satisfied with the resolution of our situation and has returned to slumber.

I will be doing no such thing. This experience definitely taught me how special every moment is that I have with my grandmother, and I'm not going to waste a moment of it tonight.

Curling up on the settee with a thick throw and the added warmth of Mr. Cuddlekins, I can't stop grinning as Grams regales us with details of her near departure.

I promise myself I'll stay awake, but as the calm of having her back, combined with the melodious hum of her voice, washes over me, I drift into dreamland with sweet visions of Grams and Odell — young, in love. Without knowing it at the time, they built a family that would one day result in me entering the world.

What if Erick and I had a child?

The dream shifts to a vision of my handsome husband bouncing a babe on his knee.

Dreams are funny that way. Everything can seem idyllic and perfect. But I love exactly what we have right now. I'm not sure I'm ready for that kind of change.

Just as the little tike is about to turn his or her face toward me, the vision slips away, and peaceful slumber consumes me.

My family is whole.

End of Book 4

But, the mysteries continue...
Curl up with the next book in the Harper and Moon Investigations series!

A NOTE FROM TRIXIE

Cheers to saving Grams! Thank you for joining Mitzy and Erick on their new adventures in **Harper and Moon Investigations**. As always, I'll keep writing them if you keep reading . . .

The best part of "living" in Pin Cherry Harbor continues to be feedback from my early readers. Thank you to my alpha readers/cheerleaders, Angel and Michael. HUGE thanks to my fantastic beta readers who always give me actionable and honest feedback: Veronica McIntyre and Nadine Peterse-Vrijhof. And big "small town" hugs to the world's best ARC Team – Trixie's Mystery ARC Detectives!

My brilliant editor Philip Newey had some great notes on winemaking. Many thanks to him! I enjoy getting his notes and polishing each case. I'd also like to give proper gratitude to Roxx at Proof Perfect for the wonderful proofing! Any remaining errors are my own.

Big thanks to Mason and Chris at Alcantara Vineyards and Winery for all the behind the scenes scoop! Winemaking is fascinating.

FUN FACT: I've actually snowmobiled across a frozen lake — lived to tell the tale!

My favorite line from this case: "Patience is not a lesson I'm destined to learn in this lifetime." ~Mitzy

I'm currently writing book five in the **Harper and Moon Investigations** series, *April Curses and May Hearses*. All your *Mitzy Moon Mysteries* series favorites will continue on — but there will definitely be a murder!

I hope you'll continue to hang out with us.

Trixie Silvertale (January 2024)

APRIL CURSES AND MAY HEARSES

Harper and Moon Investigations No. 5

Ding! Dong! The witch is dead?

Mitzy Moon is looking forward to a memorable first anniversary. Though celebrating in a snowbound land wasn't quite the event she had in mind. But this psychic sleuth must put her party plans on ice when a local shopkeeper suffers a senseless attack.

After discovering a magical talisman missing from the crime scene, Mitzy struggles to uncover further clues. And the moment she desperately needs her alchemy mentor's guidance, the trouble takes a personal turn... now she fears she could be the next target.

Can Mitzy and Erick dig up crucial evidence before she's sent six feet under?

April Curses and May Hearses is the fifth book in the hilarious paranormal cozy mystery series, Harper and Moon Investigations, a spinoff from the popular Mitzy Moon Mysteries. If you like snarky heroines, supernatural intrigue, and a dash of romance, then you'll love Trixie Silvertale's spellbinding secrets.

Buy April Curses and May Hearses to lay a villain to rest today!

Scan this QR Code with the camera on your phone. You'll be taken right to the next Harper and Moon Investigations case.

GET YOUR FREE NOVELLA!

When a suspicious death takes the life of a friend, our psychic sleuth must expose a killer's dirty laundry...

Get access to this Exclusive Harper and Moon Investigations Novella – *Ropes and Last Hopes* – **FREE**!

This Exclusive Novella is only available ***FREE*** *to members of the Paranormal Cozy Club, Trixie Silvertale's reader group.*

Visit the link below to join the club and get access to the **FREE** novella:

https://trixiesilvertale.com/paranormal-cozy-club-4/

Once you're in the Club, you'll also be the first to receive

updates from Pin Cherry Harbor and access to giveaways, new release announcements, short stories, behind-the-scenes secrets, and much more!

Scan this QR Code with the camera on your phone. You'll be taken right to the page to join the Club and get your FREE Novella!

THANK YOU!

Trying out a new book is always a risk and I'm thankful that you rolled the dice with Mitzy Moon. If you loved the book, the sweetest thing you can do (*even sweeter than pin cherry pie à la mode*) is to leave a review so that other readers will take a chance on Mitzy, Erick, and the gang.

Don't feel you have to write a book report. A brief comment like, "Can't wait to read the next book in this series!" will potential readers make their choice.

Leave a quick review HERE
https://readerlinks.com/l/3601043

Thank you, and I'll see you in Pin Cherry Harbor!

ALSO BY TRIXIE SILVERTALE

Mitzy Moon Mysteries

Fries and Alibis: Paranormal Cozy Mystery

Tattoos and Clues: Paranormal Cozy Mystery

Wings and Broken Things: Paranormal Cozy Mystery

Sparks and Landmarks: Paranormal Cozy Mystery

Charms and Firearms: Paranormal Cozy Mystery

Bars and Boxcars: Paranormal Cozy Mystery

Swords and Fallen Lords: Paranormal Cozy Mystery

Wakes and High Stakes: Paranormal Cozy Mystery

Tracks and Flashbacks: Paranormal Cozy Mystery

Lies and Pumpkin Pies: Paranormal Cozy Mystery

Hopes and Slippery Slopes: Paranormal Cozy Mystery

Hearts and Dark Arts: Paranormal Cozy Mystery

Dames and Deadly Games: Paranormal Cozy Mystery

Castaways and Longer Days: Paranormal Cozy Mystery

Schemes and Bad Dreams: Paranormal Cozy Mystery

Carols and Yule Perils: Paranormal Cozy Mystery

Dangers and Empty Mangers: Paranormal Cozy Mystery

Heists and Poltergeists: Paranormal Cozy Mystery

Blades and Bridesmaids: Paranormal Cozy Mystery

Scones and Tombstones: Paranormal Cozy Mystery

Vandals and Yule Scandals: Paranormal Cozy Mystery

Harper and Moon Investigations

Ropes and Last Hopes: Paranormal Cozy Mystery

Bells and Bombshells: Paranormal Cozy Mystery

Rodeo Clowns and Shakedowns: Paranormal Cozy Mystery

Stiffs and Petroglyphs: Paranormal Cozy Mystery

Fatal Wines and Valentines: Paranormal Cozy Mystery

April Curses and May Hearses: Paranormal Cozy Mystery

Wheels and Dirty Deals: Paranormal Cozy Mystery

Scripts and Empty Crypts: Paranormal Cozy Mystery

Christmas Catastrophe Mysteries

Peppermint Cookie Murder: Paranormal Cozy Mystery

Apple Dumpling Murder: Paranormal Cozy Mystery

Linzer Cookie Murder: Paranormal Cozy Mystery

Chocolate Crinkle Cookie Murder: Paranormal Cozy Mystery

...more to come!

MAGICAL RENAISSANCE FAIRE MYSTERIES

Explore the world of Coriander the Conjurer. A fortune-telling fairy with a heart of gold!

Book 1:

All Swell That Ends Spell – A dubious festival. A fatal swim. Can this fortune-telling fairy herald the true killer?

Book 2:

Fairy Wives of Windsor – A jolly Faire. A shocking murder. Can this furtive fairy outsmart the killer?

Book 3:

Double Double Royal Trouble – When a treat-peddling witch is found dead, will this cursed faire crumble?

MYSTERIES OF MOONLIGHT MANOR

Join Sydney Coleman and her unruly ghosts, as they solve mysteries in a truly haunted mansion!

Book 1: ***Moonlight and Mischief*** – She's desperate for a fresh start, but is a mansion on sale too good to be true?

Book 2: ***Moonlight and Magic*** – A haunted Halloween tour seem like the perfect plan, until there's murder...

Book 3: ***Moonlight and Mayhem*** – An unwelcome visitor. A surprising past. Will her fire sale end in smoke?

ABOUT THE AUTHOR

USA TODAY Bestselling author Trixie Silvertale grew up reading an endless supply of Lilian Jackson Braun, Hardy Boys, and Nancy Drew novels. She loves the amateur sleuths in cozy mysteries and obsesses about all things paranormal. Those two passions unite in her Harper and Moon Investigations, and she's thrilled to write them and share them with you.

When she's not consumed by writing, she bakes to fuel her creative engine and pulls weeds in her herb garden to clear her head (*and sometimes she pulls out her hair, but mostly weeds*).

Greetings are welcome:
trixie@trixiesilvertale.com

BB bookbub.com/authors/trixie-silvertale
facebook.com/TrixieSilvertale
instagram.com/trixiesilvertale

www.ingramcontent.com/pod-product-compliance
Lightning Source LLC
LaVergne TN
LVHW091030080826
845145LV00002B/435

* 9 7 8 1 9 5 2 7 3 9 6 4 4 *